Doing Love Right

Diana DeRicci

Purple Sword Publications

DOING LOVE RIGHT
Copyright © 2013 DIANA DERICCI
ISBN 978-1-61292-077-1
ISBN 10: 1612920772
Cover Art Designed by Anastasia Rabiyah
Photographs Copyright Stryjek and Aluha,
Dreamstime.com
Edited by Shoshana Hurwitz and and Traci Markou

Published by Purple Sword Publications, LLC
Tucson, Arizona, USA
www.PurpleSword.com

DOING LOVE
RIGHT

CHAPTER ONE

A COLD NOSE rubbed into RJ's arm, digging until he groaned. Then he was slurped by a tongue.

"Awright, awright, Samson. I got it. Daddy isn't home yet." RJ couldn't even remember how he got home last night. At least he *did* make it home. His body ached, and it felt like he'd had a rough night. Laurence and Josh sure knew how to throw a party.

Holding a hand to his head, he stiffly rolled to sit up. "You, then me," he muttered to the dog with the patience of a saint with a wagging tail. After lurching to his feet, he managed to stumble on wobbly legs across the room, aiming for the rear glass patio door. "Here ya go, big guy." The door opened and Samson was out like a shot. RJ knew just how he felt.

Blearily, he made the return trip, walked into the bedroom and froze solid, his heart slamming to a dead stop in his chest. Lying in RJ's bed on his stomach, facing away—of course—was a person he didn't know. "Shit," he hissed. "What did you do, RJ?"

His bladder prompted him to do things in order. Avoiding the bed, he made it to the bathroom, grabbing a pair of fresh briefs out of a drawer on the way. Behind the door, he held himself on a flat palm to the facing wall as he emptied himself of probably a quart or two of fine liquor. Smacking his lips, they felt dry.

Yep, drunk himself dry. He'd take a shower if he'd been alone. A splash on his face was the most luxury he could take for the moment.

First things first: he needed to see who was sleeping in Papa Bear's bed.

Opening the door, he gazed over the now-flipped body splayed across his sheets. "Oh, mama." *That came home with me?* His guest looked to still be asleep, a strong arm tossed over his head on the pillow, the other tucked under the sheet that was almost not even covering him, and RJ would bet a ten that he was cupping his cock in sleep.

A hard, broad chest, wide shoulders, brown hair, but it wasn't dark, more candied... He tried to think, his eyes locked on the sleeping god in his bed. *Caramel.* Who did he know with that color hair? RJ wracked his brain. No one who would sleep with him. This guy was as unknown as a Catholic nun at his mom's house.

"Babe, if you keep staring, I'm never going to be able to move."

RJ startled. "You're awake!" He stumbled until the bathroom door hit his ass, holding him up. The husky, sleep-drawled voice sent goose bumps over RJ. "Who-who are you?"

A gentle smile curved lusciously full lips. RJ licked his. Fuzzy memories of devouring those lips, or them devouring him, danced into his thoughts.

"Someone who's been waiting over a year for you to get rid of that lazy ass you were letting screw you."

"Huh?" he squeaked. With flat palms, he scrubbed his hands over his face, driving away the sleep and the remaining alcohol fumes. "He...you..."

Finally the gorgeous man in his bed opened his eyes and drifted to look at RJ. Rolling onto his side, he propped himself on an open hand, his elbow beneath him. Suddenly, RJ wished he was wearing a hell of a lot more than just underwear. An allover suit of armor might just fit the bill, because the way this guy was looking him over made his skin tight and his dick throb. No one had ever looked at him like the main dish of a seven-course meal. Screw that. RJ was the dessert.

He gulped noticeably. "Look, I appreciate you getting me home, but I don't bring guys home—"

"That's good to know, because you didn't bring me home. I made sure you didn't kill yourself last night after you got snookered off your ass."

He raked a hand down his face, trying to remember. All there was in his mind was a swirl of fog. "I didn't try to drive home, did I?"

"No, thank God. I'd have had a heart attack. I took a chance and went to the party last night. Finding you there made my night. Finding you drunk off your ass scared the shit out of me. You never do that."

"Wait. How do you know anything about me?" RJ still didn't recognize the guy eating him up with his stare.

Brilliant hazel eyes dropped. His shoulders rose and fell, as though gathering strength or his thoughts. "Do you remember Antonia Reyes?"

RJ racked his brain, and the brick fell into place. "Last spring?"

The stranger in his bed nodded. "My sister. You organized her wedding."

One of the few weddings RJ had accepted because he knew Antonia from years before and would have been all over her if she went bridezilla on him. *Wait.* His brain screeched to a halt. "You're Toni's older brother." A faint nod. He shoved his brain through a thought mangle, fighting to squeeze out his name.

It wouldn't come. Then a name fell from his lips. "Julian?"

Gorgeous beamed. He started to get out of bed, but RJ tossed a hand between them, halting his progress. "Not yet." He fought to hide the quivering in his legs. "Why are you here? Why do you know anything about me?"

Julian blushed. "I bugged Toni about you, and as embarrassing as it is to admit..." He plucked at the bed sheet with his free hand. "I followed you once or twice, bumped into Laurence, and, uh..." Red hued his cheeks. "Learned about the reception party. I fudged the truth a little. Said I was a friend of yours, and he invited me to come."

"Holy Christ! You've been stalking me!" RJ backed up, hiding half his frame behind the bathroom's doorway wall.

Julian's eyes widened. "No!" He sat on the edge of the bed, his head in his hands. What was left of the sheet barely covered a thigh and his man bits. "Okay, yes, but I've just been waiting for the chance to meet you face to face. Last night you were drunk, and I couldn't let you get hurt."

RJ watched Julian, misery and worry coloring his features. "Why? What happened last night?" There was something in Julian's voice. What was he missing? What couldn't he remember?

Just then the front door opened, followed by murmured male voices. "Fuck!" He glared at Julian. "Don't say a word, and don't get out of that bed."

Julian grinned. RJ rolled his eyes in answer to the unspoken thoughts in that man's head. Spying his jeans tossed negligently over his dresser, he picked them up and jumped into them. Leaving the room, he shut the door with a sharp click.

"Hi, Gregory. Morning, Charlie," he greeted cheerfully, his smile so wide, it was a wonder it didn't split his face in half.

Charlie grinned sheepishly. "Hi, RJ." Considering Charlie *had* wanted to punch out RJ's lights the night before, he could understand the shy embarrassment, but that was in the past.

Gregory set a bag down and Charlie followed, emptying his hands. RJ noticed the cane in his hand but didn't say anything.

"Hey, do you mind letting him crash for a few days with me? We're going to look for a place, but I think Dad's coming around to the new me. Dinner tonight."

RJ relaxed. This was normal stuff, friends stuff. "Really? That's great!"

"Uh, RJ? Whose car is out front and where is yours?" Gregory hooked a finger through one of Charlie's jeans belt loops, keeping him close.

RJ's face fell to his palm. "Fuck," he muttered. That explained some of last night. "I'm guessing my car is still at the hotel." He'd have to find a way to go get it.

Then, of course, more of his night that overflowed to day appeared. Julian opened the bedroom door. "Hey, babe. I'm gonna grab a shower." RJ whipped around and growled, his hands forming fists. Julian laughed into the face of his glare and shut the door on them all.

"Ohh-kay. That answers the car question," Gregory said, giving RJ a questioning stare.

Samson barked at the back glass door. "I'll let him in," Charlie offered, walking around RJ. All wiggles and tail, Samson bounded into the house, almost knocking Charlie off his feet to reach Gregory.

Samson's body vibrated with happiness to see Gregory. Madness had taken over RJ's home.

RJ gritted his teeth, fighting for calm. "Look, he's welcome as long as you need. I need to think. I'll be out in a few minutes." Then he spun on a heel and marched for his bedroom.

Of course, Julian hadn't been kidding. The shower was running in the bathroom with the door open.

He stormed to the bathroom. "What do you think you're doing?" RJ screeched, and didn't care that the shrill sound came back to him.

"Getting clean. Wanna join me?" Julian's honeyed tones raced over RJ's nerves.

"I told you to stay in here!"

"I did. I was just being polite to let you know where I'd be, babe."

RJ wanted to shove his fingers through his eyeballs. Instead, he just rubbed them really hard. "I would have figured it out, Julian. And polite would have been *asking* if you could use the shower, not commandeering it!"

A low, rolling chuckle bounced off the tiled walls. "Quit trying to throw a snit. Come here." Julian's hand emerged from the shower curtain and with a finger, bade him closer.

"I am *not* throwing a snit! I don't bring guys home!"

RJ was about to hyperventilate, he was breathing so fast.

The curtain moved and water cascaded over a round face, though there wasn't any sign of extra body mass on him. Julian had the proverbial baby face thing going on, which made him angelic and cute, and made it even harder for RJ to stay mad at him.

"Babe," Julian said gently. "You didn't bring me home. I made sure you got home." He tipped his head. "Come in here and get clean, then I'll explain everything. Okay? I'm not going to bite." A show of teeth accompanied the sparkle in his eyes. "Well, unless you ask me to, *again*." He purred the last word, leaving RJ to groan over his lack of memory.

"Why should I trust you?" he snapped.

Julian seemed to consider his answer, leaning on a shoulder to the wall of the shower stall. "Because I'm the one who brought you home, didn't let you drive, and didn't let that forty-something pretending to be thirty-year-old freak molest you when you were too drunk to know better."

Cool eyes didn't blink.

"Oh, God." RJ shivered. "I was attacked?"

"Not entirely, but two more minutes and you would have followed him to God knows where, and I wasn't going to let that happen. I heard what he was saying, and none of it would have felt good for you," he explained evenly.

Something... "A gag? *Bondage?*" RJ's shoulders bowed in as flashes of memory assaulted him.

Julian nodded. "I thought you two were hitting it off, until I began to purposely eavesdrop and heard him. He wanted to take you home and whip you like a bad side of beef."

RJ plopped down on the closed seat of the commode. "What did you do?" he asked, feeling more than a little dizzy.

"I interrupted in a big way, pulled you into my arms and stole you to the dance floor like we were the best of friends, which is where I realized you were toasted beyond any hope of return." He glanced away. "I had to look in your wallet to find out where you lived, but I got you here."

"Did we...?" Nausea tickled his throat that he couldn't remember jack shit.

"Honestly, not as much as I wanted, but we aren't hand-shaking strangers."

RJ groaned, his eyes closing.

"Babe, just get in the shower. The water isn't going to be hot much longer with all the yakking."

Numbly, RJ obeyed, standing to drop his jeans and underwear right there and accepted a helping hand over the ceramic wall. Shaky, he moved with Julian until they stood together under the spray.

"Hang on to me, RJ. Let me take care of you."

Resting his forehead on Julian's shoulder, he clung shivering as soap lathered, then rinsed down his body. The tender stroke of hands on his ass sent that tingle over his skin once more. Nothing but fingers and hands. No kisses, no lips, nothing but what he'd offered. RJ relaxed further.

"Flip," Julian teased gently. RJ did, his back to Julian's front, and closed his eyes to the caring touch as he bathed RJ from his neck to his hips. Water splashed against his chest in a heated spray, removing the chill of what had almost happened and getting any lingering alcoholic phantoms out of his system.

A drawn-out moan eased from his lips when Julian's fingers ghosted over his groin, gently cupping his balls and gliding over his cock, not intending to arouse, but it didn't matter. RJ was melting.

"I've never been with a guy who's hairless," Julian murmured by his ear. "I have to admit, it's a new addiction." RJ's heart pounded. "Stand up." RJ was guided under the water stream and a few seconds later, lather and firm fingers worked magic in his hair.

"No one..." He sighed, trailing off. "Feels good."

"Then no one has been taking care of you the way you deserve," Julian informed him. "Okay, water one more time." RJ closed his eyes, and with his hands braced on marble, he let Julian rinse away the shampoo. Julian's hands coasted over his length, touching and sweeping until every sign of soap was washed away.

"Can I?" Julian whispered hoarsely. Thumbs separated his ass cheeks.

RJ's head hung limp between his still-suspended arms. "Do what?" he managed.

"This."

RJ hissed as Julian ran his tongue down the seam of his ass. He stiffened in more than one way as sensation sliced through him on a rocket of arousal. His cock ached and filled.

"Julian," he murmured. Rivers of warm water suddenly chilled to ice as the heated water ran out. He gasped at the sudden change.

"Hm?"

"Water. Cold."

Without a word of complaint Julian stopped what he was doing. He then stood and turned off the taps. He slid the curtain out of the way and stepped out. Reaching for a hanging towel, he dried his face and then offered RJ a hand.

"Still mad at me?" Julian asked, patting the towel to his chest once they were both standing. RJ filched a clean towel out of the bathroom closet.

RJ finished with the towel and hung it with Julian's next to it. "Honestly, I'm not sure. The stalker thing still freaks me out a little."

A warm palm cupped his cheek. "Let's do this. I met you last night. The circumstances are irrelevant."

"All I know about you is your name, Julian," RJ said, peering into those hazel eyes. They weren't mirror images, but a menagerie of colors in each eye as individual as a shifting cloud.

"Then let's work on getting to know each other."

With that, he brought them close and touched his lips to RJ's, a sweet, gentle meeting. Somehow, RJ was positive he'd just been bulldozed by a professional.

CHAPTER TWO

JULIAN WAITED for RJ to finish brushing his teeth in the bathroom, kicked back on the bed with his hands pillowed behind his head. He was glad RJ had taken the story. The reality was a lot uglier.

RJ had been drunk, there was no denying that. The guy who'd been trying to pick him up had a big mouth, probably thinking aside from drunk, RJ was hard of hearing. Julian had heard every detail about what the man had wanted. Why he was picking on RJ, who was too drunk to know what he was about to agree to, bothered the shit out of Julian. He had a sick feeling Mr. Pick-Up was looking for more than a one-night-stand and it would have ended up with RJ badly hurt, or worse. Once the word "caning" was uttered, he'd swooped in.

"RJ!"

RJ had whirled, smiling, and before confusion could claim his features, Julian had looped him into a quick embrace, planting one on his sweet mouth. "Sorry. I know I'm interrupting, but I've been hustling all night to get here for my man."

"Your man?" Mr. Dom-in-a-Park-Avenue-Suit exclaimed. Some had no qualms about poaching. It looked like Mr. Dom could go either way, a touch of disbelief in his gaze about just who Julian was to RJ.

"Yeah. I had some business to take care of. Just got here. Thanks for keeping him company."

Glad RJ had been too rocked to really get a word in edgewise, he dragged him out to the dance floor. "Please tell me you were *not* going home with that guy?"

RJ blinked bloodshot eyes at him, his lips loose and his hips looser. "What guy?"

Julian groaned. He remembered that clearly. "You're fucking wasted, RJ."

"Yay!" He'd grinned and spun on his toes, lurching into Julian when he stopped. "Mission accomplished."

He didn't care who was left at the party, RJ was officially leaving. With an arm around him, he poured him into Julian's car and after some searching, dug out his wallet. He'd been a little surprised by his name but could see why he went by RJ. With the address entered into his GPS, it was only a matter of getting there.

He hadn't expected the dog, but when he only woofed once, sniffed at Julian and licked RJ's hand, he guessed he was a cool pooch.

He'd fibbed more than a little. Absolutely nothing happened last night. In fact, more had happened in the shower between them just now than the night before. RJ had hit the twilight zone before he'd oozed into bed. Julian didn't even have to stay, but it would have taken more than his conscience to pry him away from RJ's side. First, he needed to know RJ was going to be all right. He had no idea how much the man had drunk. Second, he wasn't going to desert him when his own ride was still back at the hotel where Laurence's party had been.

Julian had been waiting months to have this chance with RJ. A little hangover amnesia was nothing in his book. Besides, he only had the rest of today to convince him to give them a shot. He had to go to work in the morning, and he was equally sure so did RJ.

After watching him from a distance, and keeping that distance, he realized a boyfriend was in the picture and did some research on Toby. Julian snorted. Yeah, he'd been a dreamboat. *Fuckin' mooch.* Worked part-time when he could find the time. Didn't contribute butkis to the rent or bills, and in general treated RJ like his God-given meal ticket. A ticket that worked his ass off more days than the week could claim.

About the time Julian was going to do something about the prick, he'd dumped RJ after the New Year for greener pastures, though Julian would never tell RJ that. Not being able to comfort him after the crash and burn of their split was the last straw.

He sighed, stretching his neck to stare at the ceiling.

Yes, he'd stalked the man, but he'd also saved him. He'd planned on making first contact last night, wanting to give him a chance to recover out of the rebound zone, and had guessed a public party where he was surrounded by his closest friends would make him feel safe. Except discovering him talking to Mr. Park Avenue, he'd hung back. They'd been pretty tight in conversation, and he knew the older man was flirting with RJ. He'd been dying to do the same thing for weeks, now that he was free. RJ may have been drunk, but a part of him wasn't keen on the offer, and Mr.

Dom was pushing. Julian shuddered. He had no problem with a little play, but the man sounded like a real-life dungeon master, and RJ was his next submissive slave.

To quote his cousins: *Oh, hell no!*

Eventually, RJ would either forgive or forget the stalking part. It wasn't like Julian had been in his face, tailing him every day, more just making sure he was alive and happy, and unfortunately still with Toby.

When he left, Julian was the first to leap on that train and ride the bitch downtown.

"Thank you."

Julian rolled his head, spying RJ in the bathroom doorway. He'd slipped his underwear back on, but nothing else.

"What for, babe?"

"For being there, for bringing me home." He shrugged, causing an exaggerated hike of his shoulders. "And for keeping me from doing something I'd regret." A grimace marred his features. "I remember some of the conversation. You're right."

"He wasn't playing fair trying to get you when you were drunk." Julian patted the bed, the side RJ had slept on. "Come here, RJ."

Black hair lay in feathery layers to his shoulders, swaying as it began to dry. He had loved running his fingers through the baby-soft strands in the shower. Not thin, just fine as silk. With his finer bone structure, his gray eyes were beautiful, surrounded by a ring of thick, sooty lashes. He wasn't pretty, that was irrefutable. RJ wasn't thin either, more middle-of-the-road with a solid chest and narrow hips, strong legs and thighs that made Julian tremble inside.

In fact, taken apart, he wasn't all that, but put the pieces together and he stole Julian's ability to think, every time. And RJ had since he'd first set eyes on him during a site consultation with Antonia for her reception.

Thinking then that RJ was just a hot guy, he didn't presume he was gay. He may be a wonderful planner, able to work magic with hotels of all sizes, make any hall worthy of any theme reception or celebration, but the guy didn't exude one gay pheromone because of his chosen profession. He had more zen and feng shui in his little finger than Julian had in his entire apartment.

Then Toni had asked about Laurence and Josh within earshot and Julian's world had flipped as he'd shamelessly eavesdropped. The man he'd been silently fantasizing about was within reach.

Except he was taken.

But not any longer. He patted the bed again, enticing him.

"You're still naked," RJ pointed out.

"I only have one set of clothes, babe."

"Oh." RJ hesitated.

He held up his right hand. "I promise not to touch, pounce or otherwise lick unless invited. How's that?"

RJ's mouth tightened as though holding in laughter, his eyes twinkling. "Were you a Boy Scout?"

"Not hardly, but I am trustworthy."

RJ considered him for a moment more. "Okay. I'm going to hold you to that promise."

Nervousness radiated from RJ. *At least he hasn't kicked me out yet.* Would be well within his right. So long as he attempted to behave, things might go the way Julian had been longing for.

RJ CIRCLED THE bed, one eye on Julian, and one eye on... Well, he was only human. Julian didn't seem at all fazed by his covert staring. Didn't appear to be aware of it either. He slipped onto the bed to lie stiffly at Julian's side. He crossed his arms over his chest, leaning against the headboard, the same as Julian. He crossed his ankles. He couldn't remember the last guy he had in his bed to just talk. Toby had lived with him, but sleep and sex was all their bed had seen.

"Relax," Julian soothed, sweeping up and down RJ's features with a gentle look. He twisted to face RJ. "Are you uncomfortable with me being naked?"

RJ was quick to shake his head. "No. I mean, no, it doesn't bother me if it doesn't bother you because if it isn't bothering you and you can be like that then I can man up and—"

Julian touched a light finger to his blathering mouth. A warm chuckle calmed the erratic beat of his heart.

"It's okay, babe. I'll put on something." Julian scooted the other way, then stood. Bending over, he grabbed a piece of clothing off the floor and slid his own underwear up his legs.

RJ stared at his round ass, firm, with dimples. Julian was as tall as he was, thicker though, and darker, more naturally tanned. RJ's Greek blood was stamped into his face. He wasn't sure what kind of mutt Julian was, only that he was too cute for his own good, and probably got away with everything he'd ever done since he was a little boy, with that cherubic face.

He wiggled back onto the bed and sighed, relaxed and content.

"How are you feeling?"

RJ focused. Julian rested with his eyes closed, his hands threaded together to lie over his flat stomach.

"Better. Not as foggy as when I woke up."

"That's good. I was worried when I got you home. I had no idea how much you'd drank." Julian cracked an eyelid. "Why were you so plastered?"

RJ left those curious eyes to stare forward across his room. "Just a moment of self-pity. It's over."

RJ felt he was allowed. Last night had been Laurence and Josh's ceremony and reception-slash-party into the wee hours of the morning. On top of that Gregory's beau, Charlie, had come riding in to the rescue from Texas after a horrible split that had all but shattered Gregory. Charlie had salvaged their relationship in glowing colors, if the fact that they were only getting in *this morning* was any indication. Even after their breakup and the mess he'd caused, RJ honestly liked Charlie and was glad he'd come to fix Gregory's broken heart.

Which left RJ as the last man standing from their little wily group. He hadn't expected Toby to end things the way he had, much less *when* he had. An *artiste*, he worked his own schedule, his own hours. RJ had given him all the time, room, and devotion a man could give.

It hadn't been enough.

The gentle stroke of knuckles to his face dragged him out of the wallowing dark. "Don't give him the time or energy, RJ. His loss is that he never knew the real man who loved him. If he did, he wouldn't have left."

RJ nodded, then gulped, his mouth falling open. "Christ on a stick," he squeaked, staring unblinking at Julian. "How much do you know?"

"It's why I didn't pursue you once I realized you were gay. I knew you were involved." Julian reclasped his hands.

"How long?"

"Since Toni's wedding prep."

RJ stared. He said that with absolutely no shame. "You've been following me for over a year?"

"No. I've been following you since about September." His brow scrunched. "I tried to forget about you when I learned you had a boyfriend. Then I spotted said boyfriend with someone who wasn't you and did some digging."

RJ gasped. "He was cheating on me?" His mending heart cracked all over again.

"No, at least, I don't think he was." Julian shook his head. Relief filled RJ, but he still felt it was useless and way too late. "But I learned what kind of a worthless dead weight he was for you."

"He's a painter. He works by the whim of his creativity."

Julian gagged, pure disdain in the sound.

RJ glowered at him. "You didn't know him."

"I'd have killed him," he retorted right back. "Did he ever paint here, try to do something that might, *might*, have been construed as actual creative effort? You know, something that might have made money?"

RJ stiffened, hating the way Julian ripped away his rose-colored glasses. Silence filled the room, and he knew Julian wasn't going to step in until RJ stepped up.

"Fine," he groused. He shoved his shoulders higher. Julian, the prick, was still slouched, comfortable and obviously not going anywhere anytime soon. "No, he didn't, not often anyway."

Julian didn't press, his point made. RJ closed his eyes. He knew Toby had his faults. What human didn't?

"I loved him," he whispered.

"I know, babe. All I'm asking for is a chance." The bed quaked and when RJ glanced, Julian had slid to lay flat. "I'd hoped you'd be out of the rebound zone, but I can tell you're really not."

"It's only been a couple weeks."

"I'm greedy, selfish, and want you now, though," Julian admitted. "But I can wait. I waited this long for you to be single. I can wait a little longer for you to be healed." A moment later, Julian sat on the edge of the bed and reached for his jeans. "I'll drive you to pick up your car when you're ready. I won't leave you stranded."

"Julian?"

He eased jeans over slightly flared hips. RJ visually traced the cut over his waist and hips as he turned to face him on the bed. His jeans molded to him, scrambling RJ's brain.

"Don't go," he whispered, finding his voice. RJ straightened to hold himself on his knees.

Julian faced him. "No, I'm not fully over him, if you want the honest truth."

"Always," Julian replied.

"But I don't want you to go either."

"RJ," he said tenderly. "I want a clean shot to be with you. I won't be your rebound boy."

He lowered and softly kissed RJ's lips. Warm pants played between them. RJ closed his eyes when the support of a palm cupped his chin. Heat pooled into his blood, making his cock thicken and throb. His skin felt tight. He raised his hands, splaying his palms over Julian's bare chest. The beat of a heart beneath flesh reached into RJ, dancing with his own.

Julian groaned and RJ whined when he took away that kiss. "Please," RJ whimpered. *Please don't go. Please make me feel that good again. Please make love to me. Please...*

Craving, hunger, desire all swirled in hazel eyes. Blunt nails curled to dig into Julian's firm pecs. He hissed. "RJ." Shuddering, he put a step between them. Sucking a gulp of air, he released it through a taut jaw. "That is why I want you, all of you. I'd hoped, and even I couldn't have imagined how sweet you would be."

Julian put both hands to RJ's face. "But know this now, just because I'm not hounding you, don't think I don't want you. When you're ready to do more, I'll be the man waiting outside your door." Holding him steady, Julian touched his lips one more time, a tease of a kiss. RJ's heart did its little tap dance over his ribs in answer.

"Get dressed, babe."

Julian's request was graveled, his desire on the surface and so strong, RJ could have been burned by it. He also realized how tight a leash Julian was keeping on himself not to do just that.

Letting him go, Julian stepped away and quickly donned the rest of his clothes from the pile by his side of the bed.

If the sight of the man in his jeans had scrambled RJ's brains, the aftermath of those kisses—kisses that weren't more than touches of skin—was making him reel.

CHAPTER THREE

RJ MANAGED a whole week before the resentment hit him with a linebacker's shoulder to the stomach.

The catalyst?

A piece of forwarded mail. He didn't know what the envelope was, and honestly didn't care.

What mattered was the address on the little yellow sticker. The piece of mail sat on the kitchen table like a bad hex, waiting to be released into the world. Resentment and anger boiled inside of RJ and every time he walked by the table, he told himself he'd take it to the post office and send it on its way later, tomorrow. Then he'd snarl in fury and bitch to no one that the letter didn't deserve to reach him. That Toby didn't deserve whatever lay in that envelope, even if it did look personal, and hand-addressed.

He'd declined Gregory's intervention, offering to do the deed himself to ease RJ's pain.

RJ wanted to bathe in the blood of that pain.

Then he realized what was fueling his anger. RJ wanted answers. He wanted an explanation to Toby's desertion. Hadn't RJ been enough? Given him everything he could want? Never pressured him to do something he couldn't do? Pressure would stifle his muse, or so he claimed.

RJ was beginning to wonder if it was the muse that would be stifled, or Toby's freedom to be a lover at leisure.

RJ's work wasn't overtly stressful, but he worked long hours and just occasionally to have someone focused on him, prepare a hot bath, take him out to dinner, or even cook him breakfast...

He choked. That was not Toby. He wasn't a selfless giver of comfort. Oh, but the man could definitely suck it up like a quality Hoover. He'd charmed the socks off RJ, and RJ had continued to let him.

"RJ? RJ?" His name growing louder finally registered.

"Sorry, Pamela. What's the matter?" He lifted his head, feeling the beginnings of one of his headaches. Another backlash of past-Toby.

"Nothing. Your lunch is here."

He blinked. He ordered lunch? He couldn't remember one way or the other. "Okay. I'll be right there to pay."

"Oh, I think this one is covered."

That was when he really focused on her smirking face. He groaned, then stood from behind his desk. "Pamela, what is going on?"

"I don't know, but if you can special order me a slice of that All-American in the front hall, I'll take it."

That made no sense to RJ, until he followed his business partner to the front and was stopped cold on his feet. "Julian." Then he blushed. Could he have moaned that any louder? Only women eating chocolate-covered strawberries made that noise.

"Hey." He grinned, his hands tucked into his pockets. "Want to do lunch?"

If I get to do you, was his brain's immediate answer. His tongue thankfully didn't betray him. "I don't have anything on the planner for the next few hours."

"Cool. I know this awesome bistro. You'll love it."

RJ checked with Pamela. "You going to be okay if I disappear for a bit?"

She sat at her desk to flip through her calendar. "Yeah, I need to squeeze in a new bride at four, but other than that, I'm good."

"You better than me," he murmured where she wouldn't hear him. "I have my phone."

She waved him away. "Go. It'll do you good." A wave of sympathy floated to him. Pamela was too good to him, and kept things smooth when he had to fight City Hall or whomever over some permit or structure allowance, which could take hours.

"Thanks."

RJ led the way out of his office, down the small hallway of the office building he rented from. It wasn't uptown, wasn't high upper-crust, but he still had more clients than he knew what to do with.

"How did you find me?"

"Uh, phone book." Julian snickered, giving him a sarcastic grunt.

RJ rolled his eyes. "Animal."

"Tame me, baby," he teased quietly for him alone as they cleared the glass double doors to the outside world. Before RJ could respond, he motioned. "I'm parked over here."

"So what's the special occasion?" RJ slid into the car and buckled himself in.

"Just hanging out, lunch. Letting you know I'm still here," he added with a circumventive glance.

"I'm going to confront him." No preamble, no warning.

Julian's hand froze over the gearshift. Unfreezing and in motion once more, he nodded, then backed out of his space. "What for?"

"I want to know why he left. I want to know why he stayed. I want to know if he really cared."

Julian seemed to mull all that over. "I can see it, and understand the need to know. Are you sure you're ready to hear the answers?"

Flowing with traffic, RJ could look anywhere but at the man at his side. He'd trimmed his hair off his ears, letting it flow over his head. Encouraging him to nibble those ears.

"Ready enough, I suppose." He played with a button of his shirt cuff. "I received a piece of his mail that should have been forwarded but came to me instead. I guess they read the address and not the label." RJ had no idea.

"So you know exactly where he is."

RJ settled his head to the rest, grateful Julian wasn't berating him for his need to know. "I do."

"Does she know you're gay?" Julian asked a few minutes later.

"Oh, yeah. We've been doing this since I left college."

"Left? You didn't finish?"

RJ sighed. "No. Gregory graduated and ruled the research archives. The man is a walking translator. Phenomenal brain power. Laurence is a study mentor, and Josh is now a professor. I discovered I liked the challenge of planning more than academia or the cost, and opened the business. Pamela came to me about a year later. I think I just like arguing with the clerks at City Hall for the big permits." He grinned when he caught Julian's dimples. "Laurence and I did his wedding and reception. The hotel is an easy one to work with, and Laurence and Josh had saved for it."

"Sweet." Julian slid a peek at him, turning at the next light. "You did an awesome job. That was a rocking party."

"How long were you there?"

"Before I found you in the crowd?" He shrugged. "Thirty minutes. I really wasn't sure if I was invited or crashing, and it took some time to build up the nerve."

RJ laughed.

"This is it." Julian stopped under some large shade trees lining the sidewalk.

"Love it already," RJ said. Seeing Julian's beaming face in answer swept his problems away. He caught his arm before he could slip from the car. "Thanks. For being here."

"You bet, babe."

RJ's heart squeezed, but not in pain.

Once inside and seated, they reviewed the menus. Temperate breezes fluttered the shrubs outside, but it was still too cool to eat out there. A musical samba played over the sound system. A waiter came and took their preliminary orders and scurried away like a flittering butterfly. Decided, he set his menu on the table and watched his lunch date.

"You know more about me than I could have possibly told you, so what can Julian Reyes tell me about himself?" He rested an elbow on the table and held his chin on a fist, gazing into those hazel eyes. Bold, brilliant and always changing in the sunshine. The way the sunlight sparkled in the blend of colors made him think of fireworks. Drinks appeared before them and they gave their orders.

"What would you like to know?"

"Don't even go there," he scoffed.

Julian sipped his tea, looking into the bottom of his drink. "You're not going to laugh, are you?"

"Depends. Are you a clown in disguise?" RJ asked in his best proper accent, looking down his nose.

Julian's lips twitched. "Okay, I deserved that. I'm a registered nurse."

"Really? An RN?" RJ purred, his lashes falling to hide his eyes. "Can we play doctor?"

Julian groaned. "Smartass."

He was just warming up to flirt outrageously when the waiter brought their lunch plates. *Saved by the bell.*

"Where do you work?" RJ asked.

"A pediatrics office. I work Monday through Thursday, then volunteer at the pediatrics wing at the hospital on Fridays. I'll go later since taking you to lunch was more enticing."

RJ's hand slowed, his fingers holding a chip. "You like kids?" RJ's stomach quivered with fear. Lunch suddenly seemed much less appetizing.

"Love them." Julian beamed. "They see the good in everything. They laugh for nothing. They cry if it really hurts, and they tell it like it is." His grin turned rueful. "Not always a good thing either." His tone was rife with personal experience on that front. He took a bite of his panini.

"Oh?" RJ was still trying to adjust his thinking that Julian liked kids. He'd never expected it.

Julian must have caught onto his reticence. Large eyes peered at him. "You don't like kids?"

"Never really thought about it. I mean, they're kids, young and cute, little people who grow up and become...well, us."

"True." Julian's attention zeroed in on RJ. "Haven't you ever wanted to share what you know, give back to the world?"

RJ released his chip, wiping his hands on his napkin. He sat back from the table, staring out.

"In all honesty, no." He held up a hand. "Let me tell you why. My grandmother is the one who set aside money for me to go to school. I tried it, and thankfully didn't sink the lot on a diploma that would now be no better than me asking would you like fries with that. I saved what I could, and it's in my name. All I know about my dad is he is Greek, was vacationing in California, and was already married when he boffed my mom. She found that out the hard way, by trying to find him to tell him he was going to have a son. She got support, though he fought it. One of his stipulations was I never try to contact him. Apparently it made bad blood between his family and his wife's to have a child that wasn't, you know, theirs. No surprise there. It makes no difference to me. She used what she needed and by the time I was walking, had found Jesus at the bottom of a bottle. Grandma came to stay with us until she died. I have the entirety of my mother's inheritance coming to me. Gram didn't want her drinking it away."

He waved away Julian's words when he tried to interrupt. "I know. It's another sob story, like a million others. I know, I could look at it in a different light, but why change now? I'm thirty-three, and Mother's been in rehab twice. She can't stay out of the booze." He picked up a pickle slice and stared at it. "When you'd said I didn't get drunk, you didn't know the half of it. I *don't* drink, but I'd hit a bad low that night. My best friends had just tied the noose, my other best friend had his boyfriend come in and sweep him off his feet after a very damaging fight between them, and here I was, freshly dumped by a man whose extent of effort was he remembered to do a forwarding card when he left my ass in the dust."

"RJ, those are individual people, not every person or child out there. Some of them, all they want is someone to smile, to let them know they can be loved."

"And I applaud you and those who can do it." He shook his head. "I'm not one of them."

Shadows of disappointment darkened Julian's eyes.

"Julian, baby," RJ offered gently. "If you had pictures of a big family, picket fences and PTA meetings, then I'm not going to be a good match for you." He reached and found Julian's knee beneath the table. Julian's hand fell and covered his in answer, capturing him.

"It's not something I plan on right now, but yes, I wanted to adopt."

RJ's heart ached. "Then maybe being friends is all we can be." And damn, but didn't that idea just suck hard.

CHAPTER FOUR

"ARE YOU Sure you don't want us to come up there with you?" Gregory asked from the passenger seat. Charlie rode in the backseat, both there for moral support.

RJ stared at the house. Manicured and primped, the lush lawn was a green velvet blanket that coated the ground, even for late winter. Rose trellises lined one side of the house and trees shaded it, front and back. "Well, that answers one question," he muttered. Money. Whoever Toby had shacked up with was definitely a sugar daddy. "No," he answered firmly. "This won't take but a few minutes. I have nothing to say to the man, and what I want to know won't take five sentences."

Gregory put a hand on his shoulder and squeezed. Solidarity. Drawing his strength around him like armor, he slipped from the car and strode up the steps from the bricked driveway. He hesitated only once, making a fist over the doorbell, then preparing himself, jammed his thumb against the lit pad.

A well-dressed man in his late thirties opened the door. Slacks and shined shoes, even at home. "Can I help you?"

"Is Toby Arend here?"

"Are you a friend of his?"

"An old friend. A piece of his mail came to my place. I wanted to return it, and speak with him." RJ tapped his jacket hip pocket where the envelope was visible.

The man at the door seemed to consider RJ, his expression closed and thoughtful. "Let me find him. Care to come in?"

RJ stepped over the threshold, but then said, "I'll wait here. I won't be long."

"Your choice," he remarked in a smooth voice. He turned away and left RJ. He crossed his arms and surveyed Toby's new digs. *You're moving up in the world, prick.* RJ had never thought he was doing that badly. He had a nice condo in a good area, a larger than postage stamp-sized rear yard and a thriving business. Apparently, it was too lowbrow for Toby. Class and money elegance were prominent in the polished wood of the walls and the high sheen of the floors. RJ didn't want to see the rest of the house. He wasn't this superficial.

A few minutes later, the tap of rushed footsteps reached him. Hushed whispers flowed down the hall, and then for the first time in over a month, RJ saw Toby face to face.

"RJ!" Toby gasped as his eyes fell on his ex-lover.

"Hello, Toby."

"Will you be okay, Toby?" Smooth Talker asked, coming up behind him.

"Yes, thank you, Josiah. I'll be fine."

RJ waited by the door as Josiah gave Toby a quick, caring look, then turned on a heel and left.

"What are you doing here?" Toby nearly snapped as he closed the distance. His hair was a mess, and the not-often-encountered smell of turpentine clung to him. He was painting. RJ fought the twinge of pain. Paint flecks proved he wasn't imagining it. Toby had found his creative purpose again.

He reached into his pocket. "This came to me by mistake."

Toby took it and folded it in half without even looking. "You have to go."

"I will. I only needed to ask you a couple of questions. Can you do that, Toby? Honestly?" RJ shot a look over his shoulder, making it clear that he knew precisely who and what Josiah was to him.

Toby whipped a harried look behind him as well. "Okay, yes, but make it fast."

RJ reached for the door. "Outside, please. This is personal."

Toby groaned, a petulant put-upon sound. "Fine!" *Because the world revolved around Toby.* How could he have missed that? Some of the pain he'd been carrying dissolved away.

The heavy door shut quietly, giving them privacy.

"I can figure out now why you left," RJ stated evenly. The house spoke volumes without Toby saying a word. He examined the man before him. A month later and he was still roguish, charming, and a full conceited ass, though RJ had mislabeled that last one ignorantly. "Why did you even bother to stay as long as you did, Toby?"

He wrung his hands. "I did care, RJ. I met Josiah at an art exhibit. He's a prominent lawyer. He has connections."

"I see. A tool to get your work seen." His opinion was low and sinking farther about Toby.

"No!" Toby cried indignantly. He rubbed a ruddy hand over his features. "It's not like that.

We just started talking and he knew *everything* about what I was trying to do."

"Were you cheating on me?" RJ steeled himself for this answer.

"RJ." His hassled tone calmed. "No. In fact, I made him wait until I knew there was no chance for you and me. I am sorry for how it happened. The holidays..." He sighed, his gaze falling, then rising again, sweeping over the drive and likely spotting the car and the two in it. "That sucked, and whether you know it or not, I hated it ending like that."

"Yeah, I can tell you're eaten up by it." *I gave you everything and this was how you treated me.* Fucking rich man's house, connections RJ never would have come close to being in the same room to help him find. Yeah, Toby was riddled with guilt over dumping him like a used jockstrap. Probably left his house that morning and jumped right into Josiah's bed the night he left him. RJ began to stalk down the steps to the waiting car in the drive.

"RJ!"

He paused and faced the man he'd lived with for over a year, shoving his hands deep into his windbreaker. Was that all relationships lasted anymore? How did Josh and Laurence do it? Hell, how were Gregory and Charlie making it work? Why couldn't he? "What?"

"Just...be happy."

RJ sneered. "Happy doesn't visit anymore." Then he walked away.

He wasn't in love with the man, and the world wasn't being viewed through rose-colored glasses any longer, either. Relationships had never been easy for RJ, and it didn't matter if he gave his heart or not, he knew it would be getting trampled at some point.

He slammed the door to his car, grinding his teeth as he watched his ex vanish inside that lavish home. "Would you two mind if I just drop you off at the house? I need some time."

"Sure, RJ. Whatever," Gregory replied. An hour later, he was alone in his car, sitting on a dark, windy road, watching the play of moonlight on the waves as they rolled onto the beach, then oozed into the ocean.

Digging his cell phone out of his pocket, he stared at the screen. Hitting speed dial, he waited for the other end to pick up. "Hi, Eliza. How's Mom?"

Her soft, dulcet tones eased more of his stress. She treated both of them with such care. "She was lucid today."

"I guess we have to take even the small victories." His head sank to the top of the driver's seat. Stars twinkled overhead, yet the shimmer left him cold inside.

"Did you want to be with her for her next assessment, RJ?" Eliza asked gently.

"The doctor said if there was growth this time, the operation was a null option," he said, his throat tightening. How sad was it that his mother had been drunk for so much of her life, the pain she'd imagined as emotional, was physical. Two tumors had been identified. One was inoperable. The other was incapacitating her. She hadn't had a drop of liquor in two years, but it had ceased to matter. Her liver was riddled and she was dying, in more ways than RJ could count.

"RJ?" Eliza's voice brought him to the phone in his hand.

"Call me when you have the appointment made. I'll find time to be there." *Not that she'll know it.* She hadn't recognized her own son in almost a decade.

There were times he wanted to find his father. He could. He had all the information he needed, but he didn't. He'd made it clear where Monica Sommers and her son stood with him.

Another relationship he'd somehow failed at, and he hadn't even been aware of that one.

So, he'd struck out with his first college heartthrob, then Toby, his biological father, and his own mother. He was batting a streak.

The cell vibrated in his hand. He glanced at the number but didn't know it. Probably a wrong one. "Hello?"

"Hey, babe." Julian.

He closed his eyes, sagging like a rag into his seat. "Let me guess, phone book again?" He'd never given Julian his cell number. The house line, sure. Cell, no.

"No. Business card."

RJ groaned. He had been at the office last week.

"Where are you? The guys at your place said you weren't home yet." Why, he didn't know, but Julian sounded concerned.

"I'm sitting in my car, staring off into space, wishing."

"Oh? What are you wishing for, baby?" Julian asked, sweet as honey and as sinful as Amsterdam.

"Honestly, I don't know."

"Come over."

"Julian, you and I—"

"Don't you dare say it." Julian cut him off. "Just come over. Get yourself here and we'll take care of the rest, or let the rest take care of itself."

"We aren't a good match," he reiterated.

"And I think you're wrong, but that's beside the point." Julian sighed. "I know you went to see Toby tonight, RJ. Just come over. Come yell, or cry, or just let me hold you, but don't do this to yourself alone."

Several minutes passed with just the sound of the waves.

"Okay," he relented. He rubbed a hand over his face. "Where do I need to go?"

Julian gave him the address.

"If I get lost, I'll call."

"I'll be here."

RJ disconnected, then started his car.

RJ RECOGNIZED Julian's Mazda and parked next to it. Spying through his windshield, he hunted for the apartment numbers. He knew he should have declined, argued. There was no chance really for him and Julian. Firming his jaw, he turned off the engine. He was there now. No point in leaving. Besides, Julian knew he was there. He had to let him in the front security gate.

Slipping from the car, he took a quick inventory. A nice complex, clean. Fairly quiet for a Friday night. Hitting the lock button on his key set, he wound his way up the walk to the stairs, climbed them, then knocked.

The door opened almost instantly. He stood there in ratty at-home jeans and a pale washed T-shirt. It wasn't an image RJ would have given the other man, leisure or not. "Were you watching through the hole?" RJ studied Julian, and as he did, a faint red heat colored baby-round cheeks. RJ groaned, a short laugh on the tail of it. As though realizing they were standing on the step, Julian hopped out of the way.

"Come on in."

He shut the door and faced RJ. "Babe?" RJ swung to the softly-spoken burr of his voice, finding Julian watching him. Then he opened welcoming arms, and after about three seconds, RJ sank into them.

"It's okay," Julian crooned, running a hand over his back. RJ closed his eyes and soaked up his heat.

"It will be. I'm getting better." He nuzzled in until he was pressed into Julian's neck. "He said he hadn't cheated on me. I guess that's a good thing." RJ would still get tested. Only a fool believed in the purity of mankind, or ex-boyfriends.

"It'll get better."

"You have ulterior motives," RJ groused playfully.

"And?"

He made RJ chuckle. A sigh slipped from him as he relaxed. "I know why it hurts so much," he said moments later.

"Oh?" Julian's calming stroke never stopped.

"It's not because I still love him, because I don't, but because after all the time together, all the things I did to make sure he had time and room, he did nothing with it. Instead, he lands himself a rich sugar daddy who can move his career forward."

"It felt like a slap in the face," Julian remarked gently.

"Yeah." The scent of Julian filled him with each inhale, encouraging him to burrow closer. Warm chest and strong arms. Nothing better in the world. "I'm over him, but glad I went tonight. I needed the closure." Understanding fingers drifted through his hair, sending light chills over RJ's body.

"I'm glad to hear it."

"You know, there's no hope for you and me. I'm a relationship black hole."

"Shut up." Julian's fingers tightened in his hair, urging him to lift. Those glittering hazel eyes had softened, and watched him closely. "Stay tonight."

CHAPTER FIVE

JULIAN'S HEART was pounding. He hadn't exactly anticipated saying that, but now that RJ was there, he didn't want to let him leave. "I want to hold you, baby," he admitted, his thumb stroking over RJ's temple.

"Tell me first why you called looking for me."

Julian knew why he wanted to know. Since their lunch last week, they'd only spoken twice and nothing personal was mentioned. He hadn't wanted to push RJ after the adoption revelation and knowing he was still dealing with Toby's asinine defection. He had patience, but he wasn't made of stone. "Wanted to ask you out tomorrow. I haven't seen you since last Friday and the phone calls aren't cutting it."

Sooty lashes lowered. "Julian."

"Don't, RJ. Forget Toby. He was an ass who treated you like shit. He took advantage of a good thing." Julian held RJ up with his hand until he had to look at him. "Just stay tonight." He played with the zipper pull of RJ's light jacket, daring to loosen it a few teeth.

"That face must have got you everything you ever wanted," RJ said with a weak glower.

"Almost. I'm working on it."

RJ shook his head at the teasing. "Okay."

Julian trembled when he finally gave in. He wanted to swoop in and devour, but instead he brushed RJ's mouth with his own, a gentle sharing of heat, nothing more. He didn't want the man to think his only reason behind the invite was to pounce on him, though that had crossed his mind more than once. "Let's at least take this off." He tugged the zipper all the way down. Easing the jacket over his shoulders and down his arms, he left to hang it up in his side closet.

"It's late enough for bed, but I'm not asking for or expecting sex." Julian put a tender palm under RJ's chin. "You remember the shower?" A twitch of his lips, a twinkle in his eyes and a red hue said it all. "Will you let me do that for you again? Just take care of you for a few minutes?"

"You're an innate nurturer, aren't you?"

"For those that matter," he replied. "RJ, I haven't had anyone close in almost five years. I guess you could say I have a lot saved for a rainy day."

"It's not raining," RJ calmly pointed out.

"Do you realize you're frustrating?"

RJ's smooth lips rose, finally breaking into a cheeky grin. "Better than some other things I can think of."

"Ugh..." Julian let his hand fall. "Follow."

"Yes, Mother."

"RJ," he growled.

"Yes?" More of that innocence that was as fake as a three-dollar bill.

Julian tamped his impatience with an iron control. *Nothing worthwhile was ever won easily.* He continued to tell himself that with RJ trailing him from the front door to his bedroom.

RJ WASN'T trying to be a jerk; he was playing. What felt wonderful was he was comfortable enough *to* play. He could admit he liked Julian, but he had no intention of letting their—friendship?—evolve into a relationship. He was done with those. If it came to it, they could be fuck-buddies. Those didn't require hand holding or constant supervision, or accountability. And if one left, no one was hurt because there were no expectations. That he could do.

Following Julian's strong back into the bedroom, he lingered over his length with his gaze. The man was magnificent. Solid, but not overdone, cute but not unbearably vain. He knew perfectly well what that face could do for him. The bastard even had dimples, and not just the ones RJ had seen the morning after Laurence's party. He had deep dimples when he smiled.

"Julian?"

"Yeah, babe?" He paused a few paces into the room just ahead of RJ, tilting his head to listen.

RJ encircled Julian's waist with weightless arms from behind when he was close enough. "What if I offer?" He dragged a thumb up his midsection, scratching lightly through the T-shirt he wore.

"Offer?" Julian's voice had dropped to a rasped sound.

"Mm-hm. We aren't exactly new to this."

"Uh, RJ?"

Warm air whisked over Julian's ear in answer, his tongue flicking to roam along the shell. With Julian barefoot, his chin fit perfectly in the notch of Julian's neck and shoulder.

Tension knotted Julian's frame, his shoulders tight and flexing. "RJ, nothing happened that night. You passed out as soon as you hit the bed. All I did was strip you and stay in case you got sick."

RJ straightened. "Really? Nothing?" *But...* He tugged at Julian's waist until they faced each other. "You just took care of me?"

Unsure, Julian nodded. "I'm sorry I made you think that we had, but I didn't want you to kick me out."

"What have we done?" RJ asked in a bare whisper, searching.

Julian met his gaze, then lifted his hands to hold RJ prisoner. "This." RJ sucked a shocked gasp when Julian's lips met his own. His stare kept him still, while tender lips kept him captured. Warmth shot through him like buttered rum, sweet and intoxicating, filling his senses and his body. Longing and desire struck.

"Mm," Julian murmured. "Just like I remembered." Then he did it again.

RJ's fingers fisted convulsively into Julian's shirt. His eyes fluttered closed and he fell into the kiss. Julian took his time, creating surges of need deep within RJ. Little nibbles that lazily drifted over his lips, light flicks of his tongue that danced as he tasted. Then he molded them together, slipping between RJ's lips, questing until he opened up for the full invasion.

Julian moaned gently in answer, a low rumble that made RJ tremble. Learning caresses turned into driving thrusts. RJ locked his arms around Julian's solid torso, chest to thigh, and the meeting in between. A subtle grind ignited RJ's need into a full-blown hunger.

Turning Julian, he tipped them both to land on the bed with a shallow bounce, covering Julian. A moan rumbled upward from Julian's chest, tickling RJ's lips. Digging beneath the hem of Julian's T-shirt, he found warmed skin. Julian hissed at the contact. The thin trail of soft hair splitting his middle disappeared beneath the waistband of his jeans. Investigating higher, he found short curls under dragging nails.

"Feels good," Julian panted as he held onto RJ's hips. He lifted, grinding their cocks together.

RJ's eyes sank shut, absorbed in the shock of heat. Then he fused their mouths together again, licking and delving, tasting. The gentle strength of a hand cupped the back of his head and with a trapping leg, Julian rolled them, caging RJ beneath him. Now free, Julian yanked his T-shirt off and away with rapid tugs. RJ took full, unapologetic advantage of the expanse above him, roaming with his fingers and palms. Lightly furred skin trembled as he explored. Not thick, but scattered enough to tantalize and tease at skin and lips. RJ licked his lips anticipating that first taste.

Julian had other plans, reaching and slipping buttons free on his shirt. "I've dreamed of seeing you again," Julian said, his gaze intent on nimble fingers.

"Seeing me or seeing me naked?" RJ asked.

"One doesn't preclude the other," Julian replied. With a firm yank, he removed the tails of RJ's shirt from his slacks, finishing the last button. "Even better than I remembered."

RJ's chest trembled beneath the heat of his stare.

"So smooth." He trailed fingers down from RJ's collarbone. "Shave or wax?"

RJ chuckled with a hint of embarrassment. No one had ever *thought* to ask, much less do so. "Nothing is off limits with you, is it?"

Julian blinked, then raised his gaze. "Babe, I've asked much more personal questions. You don't have to tell if you don't want to." He put a hand to his own chest. "Maybe I should—"

RJ quickly covered his roving hand with one of his own, stopping him. "I like the way it feels. And Mr. Nosy Pants, I get waxed."

Heat made the colors of his eyes sizzle. "All over?"

RJ caught the flick of his downward searching. "Yes," he said drily. "I'm a Greek mutt, remember? I hate looking like a rug."

That made Julian snort into a laugh. "Aw, babe. You're the hottest mutt I know."

RJ shook his head, grinning. Lacing his fingers through Julian's hair, he pulled him close. "Kiss me," he entreated.

Julian lowered himself to fit them chest to chest. The raw heat and texture sent chills up RJ's spine. He didn't try to suppress the guttural moan. Then Julian was kissing him and nothing else mattered but the heat of his body and the weight pressing his ass into the bed. He widened his straddle, allowing Julian to nestle into the V of his groin. Sharp whimpers bubbled out of his throat when Julian rolled his hips into RJ's crotch, their cocks rubbing.

Blood pulsed through his veins. Julian licked, then sucked on his tongue, letting him go with a gasp.

"God damn," he muttered, his eyes dark and hazy when RJ focused on him. "Could kiss you forever."

RJ pursed his lips.

"Careful, babe. I'll give you something to fill that mouth."

"Lucky me," he retorted on a low purr.

Julian nipped at his chin, then continued to drop hot kisses along his throat. "Hm... When did you pierce your ear?" Julian tugged it lightly between his lips, sucking on it.

"Ages ago. Right out of high school."

"Playboy," he teased, licking over the shell. "Bet you were sexy."

He pouted. "I'm not now?"

Tender teeth bit RJ's earlobe. He yelped, the light sting shooting shocks over nerves. "You know you are."

"I'm not," he denied. *If I were...*

Julian lifted off his elbows to stare down at him, his hands and arms braced on either side of his head. "RJ, you are. Quit."

"What?" His brow furrowed when neither moved, his gaze locked with Julian's. What did he say?

Julian groaned and rolled to the side, an arm over his eyes. "You have got to quit putting yourself down, RJ. Toby was a fucking asshole."

"So, convince me otherwise." RJ traded places, layering over him to make a Julian sandwich.

Julian shook his head. "Babe, it's not up to me to convince you. You have to believe it."

RJ toed off his shoes. They hit the floor with muted thuds. Sex didn't require this much talking, did it? Shimmying down Julian's thighs, he admired his taut, bare stomach for a few seconds, then unsnapped his jeans.

"RJ," Julian growled.

He didn't bother to respond to the warning, intent on opening the package under his fingers. He noticed Julian really didn't put up much of a fight to keep him from excavating further.

Now that is more like it. His mouth watered as he followed that happy trail south. Unable to resist, he licked, suckling with open-mouth heat when he hit pelvis. Julian's hips jerked. He stopped complaining too. A man usually did once his cock got this close to feeling happy.

RJ buried his nose into the short hairs of Julian's groin, humming in pleasure as the raw male scent filled his senses. Then he peeled away underwear and couldn't help but stop to admire his discovery. Pulsing and thick-veined, his cock rose upward with a natural little tilt to the right. He licked his lips, then let out a pulse of air to ghost over the length, relishing the reaction. Ripples flowed upward as flesh danced beneath RJ's lips.

"God, please tell me you're clean," he whispered. He wanted that in his mouth, *now*.

"You're asking now?" RJ heard his disbelief.

"Please, Julian. Don't tease." RJ gazed upward.

"I'm clean." He'd dropped his arm from covering his face to the bed.

"Supplies?"

"Covered."

"Thank God," RJ muttered, then swooped down and swallowed the bulbous head of his cock.

Julian grunted. With determined pulls, he tugged denim lower, exposing everything without freeing the throbbing deliciousness between his lips. Gliding it all down his thighs, RJ enjoyed the feel of him filling his mouth, the slick smoothness. With clothes out of the way, Julian kicked them down and off with his legs, then stretched out naked.

RJ moaned. He'd gotten a good look at him that Sunday morning, but this was way better. Now he was touching and tasting, and...*oh, God*. He took Julian's hardened shaft deep, gulping air as flesh tickled the back of his throat. Nails gripped into bedding while RJ held him firmly pressed into the bed. Julian's hips twitched, following as RJ began the upward stroke.

Harsh gasps were music to his ears. Gnawing gently, he sucked and ran his teeth over smooth flesh, dipping into the slit with the tip of his tongue. Julian moaned plaintively. He finished with an ice cream cone lick. Shudders rocked Julian's body.

"Come 'ere." Julian's voice was raspy. A surge of pleasure struck RJ. He still had it.

And Toby was a fading memory. *Fast* fading memory.

CHAPTER SIX

CRAWLING UPWARD, he was banded by two arms, then brought down to a seeking mouth. With his lips occupied, he couldn't argue when his shirt slid from his shoulders. He moaned, his heart pounding erratically into his ribs when Julian ran learning fingers over his bare chest.

"Feels so good," Julian gasped, letting RJ's mouth free. He rolled them again, lavishing his neck and face with hot kisses. "Smell so good. Taste even better," he murmured as he licked circles around one of RJ's peaked nipples, playing with the dusky nub of skin. RJ hissed when he raked his teeth over it. Almost in apology, he gently laved over the same spot.

Julian moved south again, quickly undoing RJ's slacks. "Always so well-dressed," he remarked. "Love that about you. You're hotter than a fashion model."

RJ doubted that, but he had absolutely no strength or air in his lungs to argue. He just wanted Julian to ravage him stupid. Was that too much to ask for?

Clothing slid away, and cracking his eyelids to see, he discovered an admiring Julian hovering over him.

"Amazing." The one word held an almost reverent tone. Then he sidled up and straddled RJ's hips, groin to groin. His sac was heavy and hard, dancing against RJ. He had to dig deep to not moan in pure bliss-filled pleasure. "Want to lick you all over."

RJ trembled. Heat swarmed and rolled over him, through him. "God, yes."

Julian scooted down, pressing kisses to his midsection. RJ hoisted his hips, silently imploring for his magic touch. A low rumbled laugh eased upward.

"Soon. I can't get enough of how sweet you taste, or how smooth."

RJ whimpered. "Tease."

Julian cocked an eyebrow. "What's the rush?"

RJ growled in exasperation. Then Julian did the unthinkable. He stood from the edge of the bed and offered a hand. "Come with me."

"I've been begging to do just that!"

Julian's grin increased in wattage. He twitched his hand.

Disbelief widened RJ's eyes. "We're stopping?" *Please make it a joke.*

"Taking our time," he corrected. "I want to spoil you, not just screw you."

Why? RJ was perfectly happy with that arrangement. When it became apparent Julian wasn't budging to return to the bed, but was honestly waiting for RJ, he raised a hand and let Julian tug him to his feet.

Standing face to face and toe to toe, the press of their bodies made his pulse skip.

Julian leaned close and kissed him. Not a hard kiss, just a sharing-the-moment, tempting kiss. RJ blinked when he let him go. The subtle push and grind of their bodies into one another was making him ache. "Julian?" The man continuously knocked him off balance. How was he supposed to think at all when he kept kissing him?

"It's okay, baby. Put yourself in my hands for tonight." Light fingers drifted over his face, caressing, learning, then they swept upward to capture him by his hair and Julian devoured him. A moan echoed between them and Julian took advantage, invading to taste him with his tongue, to tease and duel.

RJ wrapped his arms around his torso, his fingers kneading hungrily into strong shoulders. He wasn't sure, but he thought he might have felt his legs tremble when Julian deigned to free him.

"That's just to remind you how much I want you," he whispered. "But if I'm going to do this, then I'm going to do it right."

Right? Do this? Oh, yeah. He'd really stirred RJ's brain with those kisses. A thumb stroked his bottom lip and it quivered at the sensual touch.

"Fuck, you're incredible. Gorgeous." A wiggle shrunk any last space between them. RJ would have climbed him right there if he hadn't spoken. "Follow."

RJ didn't even have the capacity to offer a smartass comeback, docilely trailing, his fingers laced through Julian's as they aimed for the bathroom.

"It's not huge, but that only means we have to stand closer." There was a devilish twinkle in Julian's eyes. He started the water, testing it, then offering to let RJ enter first. Once both were comfortable, he swung the curtain closed.

"Just relax, sexy," he coaxed. RJ gazed at him. What else could he do? Then Julian soaped a bath sponge and swirled it over his body. "Slick and sexy." RJ trembled, soothed by his touch, but was left simmering by the raw desire in his eyes and the sexy rumble of his voice.

RJ tossed out a hand to lean against the wall when the sponge looped beneath his heavy cock, scrubbing gently with it throbbing in tandem to the light brushes. His other hand clamped like a vice to Julian's shoulder. Whimpered mewls filled the shower. Julian crouched to soap and rinse his legs, even down to his toes.

RJ was past complaining. He was in sensory overload, unable to do anything but force himself to stay standing on two shaking legs. A shower had never been so...*erotic* in his life. Like Julian wanted to touch every inch of his body.

"Turn around." RJ did. Julian adjusted the spray. "Hands forward."

RJ moaned, his fingers tightening to claws when he dragged the sponge over his shoulders and down his back. Strong fingers kneaded and rubbed in tandem, strokes and caresses alternating with those magic massaging fingers. Soap trickled down his body, tickling him as it rinsed away. Encouraged to widen his stance, he did only to gasp. The shocking roughness of the bath sponge was gently swirled and swept over his ass and between his legs, the tease of fingers circling his rosette. He gulped, panting.

"Julian." He could barely stand. If he wouldn't drown, he'd sag forward and let the wall hold him up.

"Almost done." The showerhead moved and steaming water sluiced over his body. "I took one when I knew you were coming." He spoke near RJ's ear. "This is all for you." With a tug, he was tipped into Julian's supportive frame. RJ was as loose as an overcooked noodle, moving wherever Julian wanted him. Water was pressed out of his hair by tender hands. He'd never felt so malleable, so relaxed in his life.

He sucked in hard when Julian cupped his cock. "Damn," Julian purred. "Feels so good, just touching you."

RJ lifted weak arms and hooked them over Julian's head to stay on his feet. "More."

Julian rumbled behind him. "Trust me, sexy. We're just beginning."

RJ's brain went completely offline.

JULIAN'S HEART pounded with the way RJ melted, becoming a seductive creature with his slick skin and plumped lips. Gray eyes were dark, glassy with desire, burning with lust and hunger, hooded behind thick, black eyelashes. One of these days, he was going to take a picture of him like that, just for him, because he'd never seen a sexier sight than RJ turned on.

He leaned into Julian, his head supported by a shoulder with Julian's arms looped around him. RJ's fingers dug into damp hair, holding on where his arms curved up and behind Julian's head. Julian glided his fist up and down RJ's heavy length and felt the tremor of his need from shoulder to shin.

A long hiss of pleasure filled the shower.

"Going to turn off the water."

RJ mumbled that he heard. Reaching around him, he quickly halted the flow, standing again to recapture the sleek form in front of him. Enflamed heat poured off RJ as Julian pressed into his back with his chest. "Want to make love to you, RJ. Want to touch you and feel you everywhere."

"Anything," he gasped in a quiet plea. He tucked his backside into Julian's groin and did a little bump and roll.

Julian slid the curtain out of their way, grasping for a towel. Running it over RJ, he quickly patted them both dry, or dry enough, then tossed the towel over the curtain rod to fix later. "Out of the tub, sexy."

A faint whimper and a tremble was his answer. Then RJ shakily straightened. Holding him tight, he followed right behind until they both stood on dry ground, Julian offering a supportive arm and hand to keep him on his feet. God, he wanted RJ so bad. Julian wanted to do this right by the other man, love him, treat him like a king, do the things he knew Toby hadn't, but those raspy pants and hungry little moans slipping from those sexy lips were driving Julian insane.

Then RJ lifted glazed eyes and Julian's heart thudded into his ribs. Wanting slammed into him. A hunger that made him feel feverish and made his pulse tick like a volcanic heartbeat. He scooped a hand behind RJ's nape and pulled him close, claiming his lips as well as a gasped groan of desire that was deep and needy. Their lips mashed together as they clung to one another. RJ bumped and ground into him and Julian felt his restraint and control shattering. The firm round flesh of an ass cheek filled his palm and he squeezed. RJ wiggled, whimpering to practically climb him.

Julian released that sinful mouth, sucking in hard draughts to think. "Babe, I want to do this right." Determined, he eased a gap between them.

RJ shook his head. "Next time. Fuck me," he pleaded. Hard fingers dug into his hair and RJ made the kiss happen. A growl filled the bathroom as RJ dipped and stroked ferociously against Julian with his tongue, tracing and learning and dueling in answer to Julian's forays.

Julian had no idea there was a wildcat under those smoldering looks. Julian gripped him tight, rolling their groins together, and RJ returned it with a hard volley followed by a grunt. His legs began to move before he consciously made the decision, walking them both out of the bathroom. He halted them at the edge of the bed, releasing RJ's hypnotizing mouth.

Gasping and already feeling lightheaded with wanting, he felt as RJ's hands unwound from their fisted hold, slipping out of his hair and down his body. They drifted over his chest, lightly scoring a wake over extended nipples, the bite of pain shoving a hiss out of his chest. Only RJ didn't stop his slink south. He continued to drift down to his knees.

"RJ," he managed, licking his lips when they felt sensitive. God, he was already wild for the man. He didn't get an answer. Julian's body tightened like a strung wire when RJ engulfed his cock. "RJ, don't play...fuck!" A hand latched into wet black silk, fighting for any single ounce of control he could summon. "RJ!" He was growling now. His hips ached, refusing to move, leaving Julian crying at him with the need to pleasure himself in that wicked, heated cavern.

His eyes crossed when RJ's mouth went magical, gliding and tightening down to the root. The flicked heat of his tongue was a tease, torturing everywhere, shooting veins of fire into his body.

"Fuck!" He lurched and gripped RJ under his arms, heaving him up and tossing him to the bed on his back. He grunted on impact, swinging his hair in such a way that Julian knew it was unconscious, but was so unbelievably erotic, a gorgeous image. RJ splayed his legs and hitched a knee, just a little to plant his foot, his hard cock standing straight up from his groin.

Olive skin was warmed with lust and the heat of the shower. Gray eyes sizzled.

Julian didn't wait another second. He leaped upward, flying to land braced over RJ, capturing him with a startled gasp that morphed into a seductive moan. The bed settled beneath them. RJ's head tipped, raising his chin.

Julian rocked their bodies together, friction slicing over his spine and through his blood with sparks of energy.

"You want me that badly?" Julian managed.

"Need you," RJ replied, hoarse. "Please." For just an instant, those eyes beneath him focused, and what he saw made Julian's heart pound. So much, he couldn't decipher it all in that split second. But the *need*, the *hunger*, was unmistakable. RJ wanted deep satisfaction.

"I got you, babe," Julian whispered, rocking their cocks together to RJ's enjoyment. Tremors rolled over his lithe frame. Reaching for the drawer of the nightstand, Julian grasped the lube and condoms, dropping the packets on the bed by their feet. "Going to fuck you until you scream."

"Yes!" RJ hissed, humping upward. Dampness from the tip eased the friction as he moved against Julian's hip.

Squeezing lube on his fingers, Julian watched RJ's face. A hand clawed into the bedding and he pushed into Julian's invasion, moaning. Squirming downward, he continued to loosen him, unable to resist the glistening tip now near his mouth. Drops of fluid had seeped out and leaked down the side. He licked them up in tandem to the driving of his fingers. RJ keened when he popped his lips around the head, sucking him hard as he withdrew and inserted a third finger.

"Julian!" Pants and harsh gasps filled the bedroom. RJ tasted like no one he'd ever known. Whether it was the hairless aspect or not, Julian was hooked. Swallowing him deep, he twisted his fingers, nimbly nudging back and forth over the bump of his prostate. RJ began to jerk his hips with each stroke.

Julian let his cock go with a pop, wanting to finish him off that way, with him wailing and keening in need. *Next time.* He knew what they both wanted.

Hunting quickly for a condom, he ripped it open and sheathed his aching shaft, quickly dropping more lube on it to slick his length. Wiping the excess over RJ's sweet ass, he said,

"Turn over, babe. I'm going to give you what you want."

RJ gasped, then swung an arm until he could roll over. Julian helped him settle, aligning him. Caresses and murmurs of appreciation filled the space. "Been dreaming of this, RJ," he whispered. He'd make slow, sweet love to him next time. RJ had him so wound up, he couldn't find a new gear now if his life depended on it.

He eased forward and groaned with RJ when he slipped through the first ring. His eyes slammed shut. RJ was ready for him, his channel hotter than a furnace, and wiggling for more.

"Julian." RJ panted, his hands clawing deep into the blankets.

"More?"

RJ nodded, his spine relaxed. Advance, then retreat. Measured motions that were a combination of heaven and hell. Then Julian was buried balls deep.

"Aw, fuck," he growled, leaning into RJ's frame. His balls sucked up hard and he throbbed. His fingers curled over RJ's hips and he pulled out to grind his way home.

Sweat was gathering between Julian's shoulder blades. RJ opened his eyes, the one eye Julian could see, staring up at him, the gray so dark it reminded him of thunderheads. "I won't break," he snarled. He pistoned his hips to slam into Julian.

Julian's control snapped.

Before he could say another word, he was riding the wave of lust called RJ, driving deep and pounding their bodies together. Keening cries of pleasure wove around them. Lean muscles and skin rippled beneath his touch, RJ's head arching on his neck as he growled and cried out with each plunge.

"Julian!" RJ tightened like a bowstring, and Julian's world narrowed to the tight heat surrounding his cock, the force of RJ's orgasm sending him over the edge. Jabbed thrusts forced pulses through his cock to fill the condom as RJ echoed him, jetting in spurts. Blood thundered against eardrums with each beat of his heart.

Releasing the steel grip he had on RJ's hips, he gradually felt his world righting. RJ panted, a fine sheen of moisture on his back and over his hips. Ripples of pleasured aftershocks stole over them both, igniting each other's reactions.

With tender hands, he eased himself away and slipped from the cavernous heat, keeping the condom in place. Wearily, he zigzagged to the bathroom, disposing of it and washing his hands and wiping down his front.

Holding a warmed, damp cloth, he returned to the bed and took care of RJ, though soft sighs now replaced the keening when he cleaned him up. He toppled to his side on the bed when Julian finished. After cleaning up the bedspread and RJ's chest for the night, Julian stumbled to his feet to drop the towel in the laundry basket.

Working on autopilot, he maneuvered RJ under the blankets and promptly took his spot beside him, curling around his warm body as they fell into slumber. Julian hadn't counted on the wild side in RJ, but it was a surprise he could certainly enjoy regularly. He fell asleep with RJ molded to his chest.

JULIAN ROLLED over, expecting to find RJ to snuggle into, except he wasn't there. Blinking groggily, he listened for him in the apartment. Dull silence. Not even a peep from beyond the bedroom.

Rubbing a hand over his face, he twisted to spy the alarm clock. Five in the morning. Geez, where was he?

Sitting up on an elbow, a cold dread filled him as all there was aside from him in the apartment were shadows. RJ's clothes were gone, and Julian's had been picked up and were neatly folded on the dresser.

RJ was gone.

CHAPTER SEVEN

RJ STUFFED his head under the pillow. Someone was pounding on the front door. Samson barked, growing excited. *Hello people. Big dog, big bark.* The pounding continued.

Finally it stopped. The pounding and the barking. Gregory must have come out to shush Samson and answer the door. RJ wasn't moving. He didn't even know what time it was. He remembered waking up in Julian's bed, in his arms... RJ trembled, digging further under the pillow. He didn't know the time, only that it was after three when he finally walked in his own door. Thankfully, he'd been able to escape without disturbing the sex machine sleeping in the bed.

If he'd wakened, RJ was sure Julian would have seduced him again. Okay, he had a fair hand in the seducing. He winced, feeling the aftermath hours later. A good aftermath, but he'd never expected to stay over. And after—

His bedroom door swung open in blatant interruption.

"Go 'way," he mumbled.

"Fuck you."

RJ flipped and sat up in a rush. "Julian!" Sheets and blankets spilled around him, his pillow toppling to the floor.

"Only a slut pulls the stunt you pulled, RJ," Julian snarled, fury darkening his eyes. His chest heaved. In the background, RJ spotted

Gregory and Charlie through the doorway, watchful but there if he needed them. "Motherfucker, which one of us is it going to be?"

RJ's mouth gaped like a dying fish.

Julian didn't come any closer than the door, but he didn't need to. RJ could see his anger and humiliation clearly from eight feet away. In jeans and a sweatshirt, he'd obviously only dressed with one mission in mind. The sun was just coming up and the first week of February was still bitch cold in the early morning.

"I didn't ask for you to stay to fuck you, but you got what you wanted. A dirty fuck."

"Julian!" RJ winced, pulling back as heat suffused his face.

"Did it help you forget him? Did you get what you wanted?" Fingers curled into tight fists, his eyes narrowing. "Next time you want to use a dick, don't come to me," he retorted scathingly, spinning on a heel and exiting the house. Remarkably enough, he didn't slam the door on his way out.

RJ grimaced, stifling the pain slicing through him like a knife along with the moisture that he refused to call tears in his eyes.

"Wow," Charlie murmured, shaking his head.

"Are you okay, Randy?" Gregory walked forward and leaned on the bedroom door.

RJ dropped his head, his hands trembling in his sheet-covered lap. Knowing Gregory waited, he finally shook his head without looking up.

"Isn't he the guy who brought you home after Laurence and Josh's ceremony?" Gregory asked gently.

Swallowing thickly, he replied, "Yes."

"And you went to him after you saw Toby last night?"

RJ dug over the side of the bed for his pillow, dragging it up to set on his lap. He smoothed the case studiously, then sagged forward and planted his face in it, another muffled "yes" eking from him.

"RJ." He shuddered, hearing Gregory's groan. "That was low, especially for you."

He snapped up, determined to make some kind of defense. "Hey! I didn't make him any promises."

Samson walked up and sniffed at the bed, his tail wagging. RJ petted him dutifully. It helped him to avoid the condemning stares he knew were aimed at him.

"I just needed to forget."

"You used him, RJ. And somehow, I don't think that's how he meant the invite. Come on, Samson, outside time." The lab perked up and bounded across the room to Gregory.

Gregory closed the bedroom door and RJ flopped over onto the bed. "Fuck," he muttered.

MONDAY AFTERNOON, RJ's cell phone rang. "Hello?" He studied his calendar, penciling in a note. He needed to do a walk-through on a hotel for a weekend convention coming in the fall. He had two hotels and a hall in mind. He waited, absently writing down the convention requirements, until he heard Eliza's voice.

"RJ, I made the appointment for your mother. Friday at three."

RJ sat up, his gaze going unfocused. He pressed himself into his chair, as if preparing himself for the coming moments. "How is she, Eliza?"

"Not well today." Worry fluttered through her words. "She's not eating again."

RJ swallowed, rubbing a stiff pattern over his forehead. "Should I come this afternoon?" Mondays were his time to spend with his mother. He'd learned to not take her condition personally. He hadn't driven her to drink. If anything, his father had. But it still tore him apart watching her slowly die. After almost two decades, sobriety had come too late.

"You know I'll never tell you no, RJ," she replied. "It might encourage her to eat if it's someone other than me." The tease was meant lightly, but RJ knew the battle Eliza suffered through when his mother became uncooperative. At least she hadn't proven to have a violent streak.

He was doing his best to keep her out of a care home, to let her live and die in the only house she'd known. So far, what he was doing was working. He doubted it would last much longer, but he'd know more when they met with the doctors again on Friday, if she could continue on convalescent care at home, or if she would need round-the-clock care. He feared he already knew the answer, both he and Eliza.

Which meant his mother's time was nearing.

"RJ?"

"Hm? Sorry. My mind wandered off. Had to chase it down." He tried to lighten the phone call.

"Will you be able to make Friday's appointment?"

"I'll be there, and I'll come by this afternoon. Would you like anything?"

"Could you bring me one of those coffees I like?"

RJ's lips attempted a near smile. "You don't even have to ask for those anymore."

She sighed. "You're a wonderful son, and a good man, RJ."

RJ swallowed. *No, I'm not.* But he didn't mention his mistakes of the weekend. He was still mired in how to fix them. "See you after work."

He hung up the phone and rubbed his eyes, covering his face with his palms. He drew a hard gulp of air and fought down the gathering storm of pain. He'd never been exceptionally close to his mother. His grandmother had raised him more, until he was in his early teens. When she passed, he'd handled the burial, grateful she'd arranged it all and had left instructions easy enough for a young man to handle. He escaped to college but when his mother grew sick—not just drunk—he had to reevaluate things.

The changes in his schooling coincided with his mother's decline. He used some of his money to make sure she had the care she needed and started his business. It was partly why he was where he was and not in some flourishing downtown district. Any excess money he could scrounge together went to his mother's care. Thankfully, his clients didn't know that he essentially worked out of a hole-in-the-wall building with small offices and bad paneling. He'd lucked out with the condo. He couldn't buy the same place now.

He ensured his mother had constant care, though she hadn't recognized him since he was twenty-five. The year before, at twenty-four, the first tumor was discovered; six months after that, the second. Then the growths were defined and labeled. Cancer.

Within eight months, her memory began to slip. She went to rehab again. When he found her passed out drunk and not recognizing him in the least, he knew she couldn't be left alone any longer. She couldn't remember from one day to the next, one week to the next, and he'd hired help to come and check on her. Eliza had moved in for home care a little more than two years ago. With Eliza in the same house, Monica had zilch chance of hoarding and sneaking a drink. Eliza had cleaned out the house. The amount of hidden bottles had been staggering.

RJ wanted her to have the treatment to minimize at least some of the cells, but he couldn't afford it at the time. Luckily, by some grace of God, the tumors didn't multiply or expand. Until this last year. Financially, he could take on the burden, but the damage had been done. His mother would never fully recover after years of alcohol abuse, and the prognosis wasn't good from her last visit. More growths were beginning to form, this time in her lungs. The chance he had to do anything to help her was rapidly slipping through his fingers. He knew what they would find out on Friday. He squelched the pangs, bringing moisture to his eyes. Monica never had a chance, and no one to help her through it all.

Just RJ.

Somehow, he made it through the rest of his day. He locked the little space behind himself and Pamela, then walked her to her car. He let her chatter about her appointments, glad she wasn't expecting responses. He really didn't have it in him today to give.

Ensuring she was settled and leaving, he walked down the block to his own car. Once he was driving, he made it a point to drive through the coffee shop Eliza liked and bought her a large caramel mocha. She didn't leave the house without his mother, so treats were special for her.

Eliza was a gem, so natural and patient with his mother. Something he wished he could be more of, but he had to work to keep his mother's care paid for. He knocked on the door, then unlocked it. "Mom, Eliza, I'm here."

"In the living room," Eliza called. RJ heard her voice as he shut the door. "Monica, RJ is here to see you."

How sad is that? It broke his heart. She had to be told he was there, and then told again that he was her son. He let out the sigh of despondent frustration. Carrying the coffee, he walked into the living room. It looked much the same as it did when he was growing up. The couch sat against the far wall, with the end table and the god-awful lamp his mother had bought at a garage sale and had fallen in love with at first sight. A resin cast statuette of a bear on a log. It looked like it belonged in a hunting lodge, not his mother's front room.

Monica sat on the couch, her hands clasped in her lap, a shawl over her shoulders and legs. The new slippers he'd bought her at Christmas donned her feet. He may not feel like he should about his mother, but she was still a person, still close in his life, yet the woman on the couch didn't look anything like the woman he'd known as a child. She may have once even been pretty.

Her long black hair had been cut into a shaggy bob, to make it easier to care for. Gaunt shadows lined her face. Alcohol had taken its toll, leaving her washed out with a ruddiness to her face.

He handed Eliza the coffee with a small smile, then bent at the waist to brush a kiss to his mother's cheek. "Hi, Mom."

She blinked and stared blankly at him. It was the same routine. He said hi, then had to explain who he was, at every visit. Some days, he wondered if it would be easier on all of them if he simply didn't show up, didn't stress everyone by making an appearance she didn't understand and couldn't remember fifteen minutes after he was out the door.

Sitting beside her, he cupped one of her thin hands in his and spent his evening with two of the three women in his life.

CHAPTER EIGHT

SQUEALS PRECEDED his name and the sound hit him like a balm. "Julian!" He whirled as if taken by surprise to be tackled by pint-size kamikazes.

Three of them latched onto his legs. "Who let the troll babies loose?" he said, trying to sound fierce. They squealed and laughed.

Johnny hopped on his feet and Julian bent down and picked him up. Johnny beamed, showing off his front tooth. He said it clearly while signing the question, noticing the child watched him expectantly, "Hey squirt. How are you feeling today?"

He held up a hand and signed four letters. G-o-o-d. He was still working on words. He'd lost his hearing during the house fire that scarred the back of his head. There was little chance his hearing would heal or return, but he was still under observation.

"That's awesome." He gave him a peck on his forehead, then set him on his feet. Julian made an exaggerated show of counting heads. "One, two, three, four. Where's Tiffany?"

"She's in bed. Her chest hurts," Marlo explained with a serious tone. Julian offered hands, and they were immediately grasped.

"Well, let's go say hi, see if we can cheer her up."

The kids nodded. Julian hid his worry behind a smile. Most of the kids in the wing were burn injuries. Tiffany was a waif of a little flower. She was also an orphan. Her mother died after the car accident that had put her in the ward, and there wasn't a father on record. Tiffany wasn't a burn victim, but had been badly slashed by glass and her seat belt. She wore long-sleeve anything, the scars on her shoulder and chest a haunting memory for a young girl of seven.

Walking through the double doors with the kids at his side, he felt some of the pain he'd been wrapped in all week vanish. He was still stinging from RJ's treatment last Friday night, or, he guessed, early Saturday morning would be just as good too. Julian hadn't called, but then neither had RJ, not that he was expecting him to. Julian wasn't sure if he'd misread RJ all those months or if it was something else.

What did he really know about him? He worked hard. Who didn't? He had a family background, a troubled childhood. Okay, Julian could understand that. He saw children constantly in varying degrees of familial problems at the doctor's office and here at the hospital. It didn't take a crystal ball to see it had scarred him.

Trying to convince himself that it been an error, an infatuation that had blown up in his face, wasn't working. If it were, he'd be able to forget the sexy Greek.

He missed the bastard, which depressed him for more reasons than he cared to admit to. He'd liked RJ, maybe too much if he was blinded to that kind of self-serving behavior.

While their first time hadn't been quite the way he'd pictured, it had still been phenomenal, blown his mind in more than one way. RJ had a wild streak that he wouldn't have imagined under those pressed pants, sharp shirts and blazers. Cool and confident, with a dash of wild. He rather liked a man that he couldn't break, but also appreciated a more caring touch. Julian couldn't stem his nature, and that was to take care of people. Thinking about the showers they'd shared made his pulse thicken and his skin warm.

A squeal and a teased pout clanged his thoughts to a dead stop. Thankfully.

He brought his attention to the hospital and his current entourage. It would not do him well to have his thoughts too thoroughly exposed. That was one conversation he was *not* having with any of the kids.

He shooed the ones holding on to go play so he could say hi to Tiffany. She was lying on her side, facing away, which told him the mood she was in. She was terrified the hospital was going to send her to some strange orphanage or foster care without family to care for her. She was still healing, though her physical injuries were the least of her problems.

"Hi, princess," he greeted, sitting on the chair at her bedside.

She ignored him, looking beyond him.

"Wow," he grumbled with mock severity. "Not even princess today, huh?"

Tiffany tucked fingers between her knees, her others beneath her cheek. Soft blonde hair curled over her ear and down her shoulder, and big-as-the-open-sky blue eyes stared at nothing. He made it a point to not cross emotional lines with the kids, because they didn't stay there forever. They had families, homes, parents and siblings.

Tiffany had none of that. She'd been in the kids' wing for the last two months. No one came to visit her. All the doctors and nurses did their best to help each child to meet their needs and to the best of their abilities. Tiffany was a case unto herself.

"Princesses are beautiful," she finally whispered, still not looking at him.

His eyes shot wide in overdramatic shock. "Then you have to be one," he said clearly. "Because you are."

She blinked and swallowed. A single tear fell from her eye. "No, I'm not. Garret's brother said scars are ugly."

Julian bit his tongue, and refrained from scowling in Garret and Marlo's direction. Garret's older brother was an ass, a nut who didn't fall far from the asshole tree. Julian had met Garret's father. Enough said.

"Princess, you know people all over look different in all kinds of ways on the outside," Julian said soothingly. "What matters is the person on the inside."

Her lips quivered. "Then why does he say Johnny's scars make him ugly too?"

Julian ground his jaw. He couldn't come out and say the truth, that Garret's brother and father were utter assholes and inconsiderate on top of it. At some point, it became taboo to discuss people honestly with children, hell, with other adults, leaving them to find out the truth by themselves. Personally, Julian felt that was a disservice. If there's an ass in the building, warn the kids. Not every person's opinion was spun out of gold and rainbows. Least of all Garret's father's.

"Tiffany, look at me, princess." She wiped at the tear clinging to her eyelashes, then finally, reluctantly, did. "Imperfections do not make us ugly. Lying, cheating, being cruel, those make you ugly from the inside, and it shows. The world is filled with imperfections. Do you know what the Sphinx is?"

She shook her head.

"It's a huge statue in Egypt, another country far from us. It's magnificent with large lion paws, and the carved face of one of their ancient pharaohs, but you know what?"

She stared at him.

"Someone, a long time ago, shot his nose off." His eyes widened in disbelief, then he covered his face to talk with a nasal sound. "You can imagine how he talks."

She giggled.

"But this statue is thousands of years old, and still to this day is considered one of the most beautiful landmarks of our world. And you know what?"

Tiffany shook her head, completely enthralled.

"He has no nose!"

She gaped. "No nose? At all?"

"Nope. So you see, imperfections like scars or blown-off noses," he gestured, cupping his nose to make it vanish and she giggled again, "are just that. They make us who we are. Some people have short fingers, or ears that don't quite match, or like me, eyes that aren't identical. Believe it or not, I have a few scars too."

"You do?" She began to sit up, tugging her Hello Kitty nightshirt around her body.

"Are you kidding? I was a boy with a mission. I jumped my bike over everything I could find, from curbs to homemade bike ramps. I have scars on my knees, even a bad one on my calf. Want to see it?" When she hesitated, he said, "It's really old and faded. It's what yours will do over time, too, Tiffany. Our bodies are always changing."

She crossed a hand to her right shoulder, cupping it. "Okay."

He leaned over and gathered his pants leg. "See this?" He dragged a finger from his ankle up about four inches, tracing the thick faded marker of his childhood. "I needed stitches."

"How old were you?"

"I think about eight. It's been a while."

She smiled when he grinned.

He dropped his scrubs leg. "Scars don't make you ugly or beautiful, redhead or blonde. What is inside makes us beautiful, and I know you're gorgeous."

She hiccupped a giggle, then let it out. When she leaned forward, he scooped her up to sit on his lap.

"But what if he says it again?" she whispered, tucked into his arms.

"Honey, he's going to do it because he wants to hurt you. Remember what I just said about being cruel, how it makes people ugly? Think about what he says, and how he says it. Is he saying it to make himself more important? Make you feel worse? Then it's not you who is the ugly one," he finished quietly.

"I think I understand."

"Good. Now, you ready to come play some Chutes and Ladders?"

"Yes!"

He smiled. "That's my girl."

He doubted a tenth of that made sense, but someone came and talked to her, just to her, and he knew that was half the need. Though if he ran into Garret's family in the near future, there was a good chance he wouldn't be quite as nice. A real good chance.

RJ WAITED in the small cubicle with his mother, Eliza in the other chair reading a magazine. The first batch of blood work had been taken to the lab; now it was a waiting game.

The curtain shook. "Mr. Sommers?"

RJ stood. A young doctor walked in. He scooped up a chart and made room for an intern with a wheelchair. "Hi, I'm Dr. Earl. We're going to take your mother down for her follow-up X-rays now."

"Okay." He turned to face the woman on the examining table. "Mom, do you want Eliza to go with you?" Eliza had set down her magazine as well as soon as the curtain had twitched, waiting. He didn't offer to go himself. He wouldn't be able to keep her calm if something confused her. Being with Eliza day in and day out gave her some sense of stability.

"Eliza?" Her fingers twisted on her lap, her dull eyes widening as she searched.

Eliza leaned over and patted her arm. "I'm right here, Monica."

His mother turned in her direction and after a moment nodded.

"I'm going to go get a coffee. Would you like one, Eliza?"

The intern who had followed the doctor in locked the wheelchair in front of him and helped his mother step down and sit.

"I'm fine, RJ. Thanks."

"It should take about half an hour and we can meet you back here then."

RJ nodded at the doctor's words. "I'll come back here for her."

"Sounds good. All right, Ms. Sommers, ready to go?"

She hunted, then calmed when she saw Eliza. "I'm ready."

RJ watched the procession leave, leaning on the wall and rubbing his eyes. The decline was growing obvious. She'd lost weight in the last few weeks, not eating. He didn't have high hopes for today's visit. Once they were out of sight, he turned the corner from the cubicle and went down two floors to the cafeteria. He'd been there so much over the last two years, he knew each floor by heart.

With a coffee in hand, he walked to an open table near a window but didn't sit. He gazed out onto the yard, following as patients walked or sat and chatted, or just enjoyed the midday sunshine. It wouldn't be spring for a couple more weeks, but the coast was balmy enough almost year-round.

Glancing at his phone, he noted it had been almost thirty minutes. Tucking it in his pocket, he left the window and tossed his half-full cup of lukewarm coffee when he walked by a disposal.

Walking out of the cafeteria, he heard laughter coming from down the hall beyond an architectural stone mosaic that created a blind bend in the hall. If he'd had warning, he might have slowed, or turned around, but luck wasn't on his side.

Walking with two female nurses, who were laughing their asses off, was Julian.

CHAPTER NINE

RJ STAGGERED to a stop. *Damn.* He sighed inwardly. The man still made his heart flutter. Looking forward, it was almost comical how their eyes zeroed in on each other.

"RJ," Julian said, shocked and whispery. The two ladies at his side shared a glance, but neither man paid the nurses the least bit of attention.

Julian blinked, breaking the spell first, tearing his gaze from RJ's to one of the nurses. "Alyssa, could you go ahead?" he asked quietly.

"Sure. Come on, Tina. Don't want to miss the cake." They flowed beyond him, their heads together, talking in low voices.

He closed the few feet between them. "I didn't expect to see you again."

RJ flushed. He knew he'd been an ass. "I'm here with my mother."

Julian deflated. "Oh. Well, then, I'll let you get back to her." He went to stride past him, but RJ reached out and gripped his arm.

"Can we talk?" he asked, wondering how much longer his heart was going to be lodged between his ribs.

Julian hesitated, intense eyes boring into his own. "I can spare a few minutes."

RJ knew he deserved the cold shoulder. Didn't mean he liked it, though. Nodding, he asked, "Where?" He let Julian's arm go, releasing him with a light sweep of fingers. Julian didn't so much as blink at the gesture.

Julian glanced around, then tilted his head. "This way."

RJ followed as he wound them down the hall and through an access door that abutted the walkways outside.

Julian crossed his arms over his chest, his pale green scrubs moving with him. "I'm on lunch, so say your bit."

RJ dropped his hands into his pockets, curling his fingers around his keys. Gazing into Julian's expression, there wasn't a lot of room for anything less than an apology.

"I'm sorry. I treated you like shit, and it wasn't right, or fair to you." He watched as a car crawled past to roll over speed bumps in the parking lot.

"You used me, RJ," he replied, bending closer, though not really shrinking the space between them.

"I..." He swallowed. God, he'd never been good at apologies. RJ should've known Julian wasn't the kind to do the fuck-buddy scenario. RJ certainly hadn't thought to run it by him first either, to see if he was on the same page. The man was too kind for it, too caring. He'd misjudged, and misused him. Hopefully, RJ wouldn't get too used to the taste of crow. "I know," RJ finally managed. "I'm sorry. I don't blame you for not calling."

"Why didn't *you*?"

RJ met his gaze. Not quite as hostile, but still not warmed. At least they could part on better terms, if nothing else.

"I suck at apologies, and I honestly didn't think you'd ever want to talk to me again. I wouldn't have blamed you," he finished.

Julian's shoulders rose as he debated, looking beyond RJ. When it didn't seem Julian was going to add more, RJ said, "I hope you can forgive me, Julian. I know it's not much. I was a scumbag for doing that to you. Believe me, I've been a mess all week."

"You and me both," he uttered.

RJ swept up to search him. A light breeze flipped through his hair, swinging the caramel strands around to toss over his forehead. Why the hell did he want to nibble on those ears? The man probably hated him.

"I like you, RJ," Julian said, letting his arms fall. "But I won't stick around for a selfish jerk."

That snapped his focus back to the moment, and away from those cute earlobes. "You like me?"

Julian rolled his eyes. "Jesus on a stick, man. I hunted your ass down at your best friend's reception."

"Stalked," he corrected, a playful twist to his lips, hoping Julian would hear the tease behind it.

"Rescued." Julian moved an inch or two closer. RJ's skin flushed under his shirt. His cock twitched in answer.

RJ licked his lips. "Julian?"

Julian's larger frame shifted, bridging the gap between them, nearly chest to chest but not touching. It was torture for RJ. He couldn't think of any other person he'd reacted to like this. Toby had been hot, able to hit all the right buttons, but Julian could do the same without even touching him. With a look, a word, Julian had RJ's heart running for the quarter mile marker at a record speed. Any thoughts of keeping things light and for fun between himself and Julian went out the window with one glance.

"Yeah, babe?"

A shiver slid down his spine at the husky endearment. "Can we try this again?"

"On one condition."

RJ considered him. He owed the man that right. He was the one who had ground to make up. "Okay."

"You ever go jerksville on me again, and I'm done."

"I can't promise I won't be a prick, Julian, but I can promise to work on it for you."

Julian studied him, his lips lifting and pinching. Then, "Okay. At least you're being honest about it." He raised a hand and threaded it through the hair at his temple. "I forgive you, you ass."

RJ sagged with relief, a smile warming his lips. "Thank you." His phone rang. "Shit!" He dug it out of his pocket and hit the keys to answer. "Hi, Eliza."

"RJ? Are you coming back? The X-rays will be here in about ten minutes."

He rubbed his eyes, nuzzling into the full-palm caress Julian was now giving him. "I'm sorry. I'll be right there."

He hung up. Sadness welled up inside and he couldn't keep it out of his voice. "I need to get back. Mom..."

Concern crossed his brow. "RJ? What's the matter?"

"It's Mom. She went for X-rays."

"Is she hurt?"

RJ shook his head. Tremors of soothing heat were drifting over his frame from the calming circle Julian was making with his thumb at his temple. "She has cancer. She's declining."

"RJ." He wasn't expecting it when Julian's arms wound around him and embraced him. "Why didn't you say something?"

"No one really knows." He buried his face into Julian's shoulder, grateful for the support. He accepted the strength while he was at it. "I need to get back to see what the doctors have to say."

A warm hand cupped his face and brought him up. "I'm off at six. I'll call, if that's okay?"

RJ nodded. "I'll be home by then." He tipped his chin. "You better go eat. I already took too much of your time."

"Shut up," he chastised lightly, just before he brushed tender lips to his forehead. "Can't kiss you the way I really want, but I'll make up for it tonight." He put firm hands on RJ's shoulders and created space between them. "Call me if you need to. I can spare a few minutes."

"Okay."

Using his access badge, Julian unlocked the door they'd exited by. A touch on RJ's shoulder made him pause. The door shut. He waited expectantly as people flowed by them, the mechanics of the hospital in motion around them.

"Tonight?"

RJ nodded. "Come over if you want."

He leaned close to whisper in RJ's ear. "And for the record, I missed you too, babe."

His heart caught in his throat, the drawled words dancing over his ear. A shiver sliced over his shoulders. Before he could drown completely in the feeling, Julian stood straight and removed his hand. A couple quiet minutes helped to derail the flow of blood south.

"See you tonight." Then Julian was walking away headed for the cafeteria. RJ desperately wanted to follow, to not have to face the coming moments, but knew there was no choice.

Spinning on a heel, he returned to his mother and Eliza.

JULIAN KNOCKED on the door, immediately hearing the lab's greeting bark.

"Hush, Samson." RJ's voice admonished the dog. There was a pause as the metallic click of a lock echoed, then the door opened. RJ's drawn face attempted a smile. "Come on in. Ignore the slobber machine."

Julian walked through the door and offered a hand to let Samson sniff, then he rubbed the side of his head. A wagging tail said he was making progress. "Nice dog."

"He's Gregory's, though he's pretty much adopted all of us."

"All?" Brown doggy eyes perked up when he spoke.

"Gregory and Charlie are staying with me for the time being."

Julian had a memory of others being at the house when he'd come last weekend, the same two he'd glimpsed through RJ's bedroom door that Sunday morning, which now seemed like ages ago.

"They're here?"

"Not at the moment."

Julian noticed RJ's hair was messed up, like he'd been running his hand through the length, and he looked more tired than he had that afternoon. What happened in the last four hours?

RJ leaned against the closed door. He wore the same button-down shirt he'd worn earlier beneath his blazer, with the tails untucked and loose, and the same charcoal gray slacks, though no shoes.

"You look exhausted, babe," Julian said.

"I feel exhausted. They're keeping Mom overnight to run more tests. Her X-rays..." He paused, swallowing, his hands hidden behind his back between himself and the door. "The prognosis is bad."

Julian reached out and tugged him off the door into his arms. A shudder rocked RJ's frame. "It's okay, babe."

"They're giving her less than six months," he choked out.

Julian groaned, hugging his trembling body tighter. RJ encircled his waist and held on.

A few minutes later RJ raised his head, his complexion wan and spotty. He swept a hand over his eyes. "I knew it was coming. I thought I was ready to hear it."

Julian palmed the side of his head and massaged him, running circles over his scalp and temple with strong fingertips.

"Come on." RJ didn't argue when Julian straightened, taking him by a hand to guide him to the bedroom. "You need a few minutes to recharge." RJ didn't balk at all when he started to unbutton his shirt. "Take this off, and finish undressing. I'm going to run you a bath."

"I didn't think it would hurt this much," he whispered. "She doesn't even know who I am."

"Shh." Julian flitted a gentle kiss to his mouth. "It's okay. Let's get you unwound, okay, baby?"

Numbly, RJ nodded. Julian left him to fill the tub. It was bigger than his at the apartment, a garden tub, he thought, or something. Hunting the shelves and cabinets, he came up empty to put anything in it to help him relax. Under the sink, he found two candles.

"Okay, then, candles it is," he said to no one. He set one on the back of the tub and the other near the sink. He scrounged again and spotted the lighter where it had been pushed to a wall.

After testing the water, he shook off his fingers and returned to the bedroom. "Come here, baby." RJ, in answer, clasped his outstretched hand. "Let's get you in the tub, then I'll see what I can do about dinner."

"You're going to cook?" RJ asked distantly.

"I've been known to scramble a few eggs," he teased back. "If you don't mind."

RJ shook his head. "If you can make it, I won't stop you."

"Easy going in. It's hot."

RJ hissed, then sighed as he sunk beneath the steamy water. Once he was settled, Julian lit the candles and turned out the light. "Rest for a while, babe. I'll come get you in a bit."

He nodded, his eyes closed, sinking lower. Olive skin grew reddish from the heat, though RJ didn't seem at all distressed by it. Leaving him with the bedroom door closed, Julian went to the kitchen.

Investigating the refrigerator and cabinets, he assembled the ingredients for a decent comfort food dinner, provided RJ wasn't too picky. Samson came over to investigate, and he gave him a friendly pat. "Okay, fella. Let's see if I remember how to do this."

Twenty minutes later, the pan of noodles was in the oven to bake. He rinsed out the pot he'd used to prep the meat and vegetables in, setting it to the side to drain. He drew a deep breath to sniff, and his stomach rumbled. "Not too shabby for being rusty."

Opening the door to the bedroom, he approached the bathroom to find RJ resting with his eyes wide open staring at the ceiling. "You didn't tell me you've mastered how to sleep with your eyes open."

"Ancient Chinese secret," he drawled. He rolled his head toward the doorway. Shadows from the candles flickered over the walls and over his features, giving him a ghostly grayness. "How is it I'm always coming up naked around you?"

"Um, my good luck?" Julian replied, leaning on a shoulder to cross his arms over his chest.

RJ harrumphed a sound. Lifting his hands, he wiped them down his face, then sank to dunk himself, coming up dripping. Clearing his eyes, he said, "I guess I better come get dressed before the other two get home. They still give me crap for waking up with a stranger in my bed."

Julian grinned. "At least he's not a stranger any longer." He plucked a towel off the waiting shelf and held it up. "Want some help?" He leered playfully, waggling his eyebrows. RJ groaned, a small smile almost breaking loose. *Better than nothing.* Julian would take it.

Surprisingly, RJ released the drain, then stood, stretching out his arms. Sleek skin made rosy red from the soak evoked all kinds of delicious, teasing ideas. Most of them including Julian's lips and tongue licking up each stray drop and wet trail left behind.

He leaned over and blew out the candles, then began to gently pat and buff all that wonderful skin dry. RJ stepped out of the tub and waited patiently. Wrapping his fingers into the towel, he even took a few minutes to massage his scalp under the guise of drying his hair. RJ sighed and leaned into his chest.

"Thank you."

Julian tilted his chin to look into gray eyes. "You're very welcome." He wrapped the towel around him. "Go get dressed. I need to check dinner."

Julian went to step out of the bathroom to give him space and privacy, but RJ stopped him. Glancing behind his shoulder, RJ landed a kiss to his mouth. "I'll be right there."

Shadows still clouded RJ's gaze, though at least now he didn't look like a feather would make him shatter. Julian blew him a kiss, then left him to dress.

CHAPTER TEN

RJ SLIPPED on a pair of jeans and a heather gray loose long-sleeve T-shirt. Shaking out his hair, he let it fall where it wanted, which meant it was going to curl at the ends. One of those Greek gifts from his father's side, he supposed. His mouth watered as soon as he opened the bedroom door.

"Wow. That doesn't smell like omelettes."

"I hope you don't mind what I used."

"Are you kidding?" He sniffed deeper, humming appreciatively. "Where did I have pasta noodles?" Gregory must have bought them, because the only kind of noodles RJ really trusted himself to make was macaroni and cheese.

"In the cabinet." Julian walked up and wrapped his arms around RJ's waist when he reached the kitchen. "It's a little light on cheese, but it's almost heated through."

"That's okay." He leaned into Julian's embrace. The front door unlocked and Samson bounded up to it with his tail wagging. RJ hung on tighter, keeping Julian where he was when his arms loosened.

The door cracked open, but their argument could be heard easily. "Charlie, for heaven's sake, the man gave you a compliment." The door opened completely, Gregory entering with Charlie following.

"He was flirting with you!"

Gregory groaned. RJ watched as his eyes drifted closed in pleasure. "Oh, man. That smells incredible. RJ!"

"I'm right here, idiot."

He whirled. "Oh." Then he noticed Julian. "Is that something I need to break up, or take bets on?"

"Fuck off," RJ grumbled.

Charlie smacked Gregory's shoulder and he winced, muttering. "He's the epitome of tact, I know. Hi, Julian."

RJ felt Julian's body tense. "Uh, hello."

"Gregory is the mouth, Charlie is the sanity," RJ supplied. He ran his thumb up and down Julian's spine, feeling him relax in measures. "Do you guys need some help?" RJ helped them refocus their attention to the bags in their hands rather than the man standing in his house, who was wrapped around RJ and vice-versa.

"Nah, we got it," Gregory said. "Rover's chow is all that's left, and I'll get that later."

"I thought his name was Samson," Julian wondered aloud.

"It is, but if you mention his name and food, he thinks he's getting fed." Gregory and Charlie came into the kitchen and dropped the grocery bags on the floor. Reluctantly, RJ let Julian go.

"Who cooked? It smells wonderful." Gregory tried to peek in the oven, hitting the inside light to be nosy like a little kid waiting for cookies.

"Julian did."

Gregory lifted an eyebrow, looking in their direction. "Damn. He's got me beat."

"Yeah, but you make the *best* burgers," Charlie offered, dropping a kiss to Gregory's cheek when he stood straight. Grabbing things out of the bags, Charlie began to fill the cabinets.

RJ rubbed his forehead against Julian's neck, wallowing shamelessly in the contact.

"Hey, we're not interrupting something, are we?" Charlie asked, holding cans of tuna fish. "I mean, Julian's here, you're not killing each other, and he cooked."

RJ choked a short laugh, still hiding in Julian's shoulder. "Would it really matter?"

"Would you like to eat with us?" Julian asked, ignoring RJ's mumbles. "There's enough for four, easily." He leaned close and whispered in RJ's ear, "It's okay, babe. You need your friends tonight."

RJ leaned far enough away to stare into those earnest eyes. "Does that include you?"

"I would like it to."

Feeling a heavy weight lift, he said, "Yeah, that's fine with me."

That crazy flutter that only Julian created hit him square in the chest when his gaze softened. With a light touch of lips, Julian's hands dropped away. "Do you have any bread? I can make toast to go with it."

Gregory shuffled through a few bags at his feet. "I bought hoagie rolls for later in the week."

"Those will work."

Within minutes, Julian, Gregory and Charlie were bantering like he'd always been a part of their group makeup. RJ opened the fridge. "Sodas or water? I can make tea."

"Tea sounds great," Charlie replied. With something to do, RJ was able to keep his thoughts from running too far amok or getting too depressed with thoughts of his mother.

IN ALMOST no time, it seemed, they were seated at the table, enjoying Julian's version of a baked ziti.

"More cheese next time," he mused, devouring another mouthful. He watched RJ out of the corner of his eye, glad he'd been okay with inviting his pseudo-roommates to eat with them. The more distance RJ could put between himself and this afternoon's news about his mother would make it at least marginally easier to discuss.

"Did you use the sausage?" Charlie licked his lips, striving for a dollop of sauce at the corner of his mouth.

"Here." Gregory lifted a thumb and stole it, popping the prize between his lips.

Charlie scowled at him. "Hey! That was mine."

"Mine now," he sniggered smugly.

"I'll get even," Charlie threatened with a glare.

That threat only doubled Gregory's smirk. "I'm counting on it."

When Charlie looked in Julian's direction, stoutly ignoring a grinning Gregory, he answered the question. "Yes. I've made it with different kinds of meat. Just depends on what is on hand at the time. Though if you guys were shopping, that explains the thin spots."

"Yeah, it was our week and we didn't get to go before now. I'm not a great cook, I leave that to these two. RJ is the one who keeps us from starving."

"Yeah?" Julian slid to look at his side, where RJ was quietly finding the bottom of his plate.

He took a sip of tea, then wiped his mouth on a napkin. "I'm not claiming any titles or perfectionism," he explained. "But I know enough to not burn water."

"So I guess you two have made up, or signed a truce or something?" Everyone stilled. "What?" Gregory glanced around the table.

Charlie dropped his face into a palm. "What is with your mouth lately, Gregory?"

Gregory winced.

Julian chuckled. "It's okay. I understand." He leaned into his chair, dropping a hand under the table to rub lightly over RJ's thigh. "I imagine I made quite the entrance last weekend."

"You could say that," Gregory agreed, meeting his stare head-on. Julian caught that out of the two men, Gregory was the closest friend to RJ. He didn't take his protective defense of RJ personally.

"Yes, we made up," RJ said, placing his fork by his plate, his head down. "Excuse me?" He stood and walked to the bedroom, the door partially shutting.

"What was that about?" Charlie seemed just as stumped as Gregory, watching the usually vivacious RJ leave like that.

Julian was at a loss. RJ had said no one really knew about his mother and Julian didn't want to give away more than the man himself had. He knew what had stolen the small level of energy RJ had. Being reminded of today, where they'd made up and why.

"I'll be right back," Julian said, standing to follow the other man. He pushed open the door and found him sitting on the edge of his bed, his face in his hands. "RJ? Babe?"

A shudder rocked his frame.

Julian walked up and sank to his knees in front of him. "Why haven't you ever told them?"

"Because I didn't want to answer the questions," he replied, a thick hoarseness making his voice raw. "And there would be a fuck-ton."

"Baby." Julian gathered him and he rested RJ's forehead to his shoulder. "You need their support. They're your friends. I think they'd understand enough to respect your privacy and still help you. You've known them for years, right?"

"Gregory, yeah."

Julian swept the hair away from RJ's face to see his expressions. "I'll help you, too," he whispered.

RJ stayed still for several minutes, and Julian let him, doubting he knew every thought roaming through his lover's mind, but sure he could nail a few on the first try.

"They should know something. I'm going to be a wreck for a while."

Julian cupped his chin and supported him, kissing his lips lightly, then his temple. Then he stood and offered RJ a hand, who weakly clasped it, letting Julian bring him to his feet. "It's going to be okay," he said, soothing RJ with a hand sweeping up and down his spine.

"Eventually." He gave Julian a squeeze with a warm kiss below his ear. "I'm okay now."

With an arm around RJ's waist, he guided him to the table again and let him sit, Julian doing the same.

"Is everything okay, RJ?" Gregory asked.

RJ pushed his plate forward. "Yes and no. Between me and Julian, we're working on it."

"That's good to hear," Charlie offered with a note of approval.

"Gregory," RJ began. "I've told you my mother and I never really got along. That's not exactly true." Folding his arms on the table, Julian listened as RJ detailed his mother's illnesses and brought him up to date with her current problems.

Silence sank heavily between the four when he was done.

"Wow," Charlie murmured. "What can we do to help?" His fingers tapped a rhythm lightly on the tabletop.

"Honestly, right now, I don't know." RJ cupped his elbows, slouching some. Julian spread a hand over his shoulders and casually rubbed. "I'll know more in the morning, but the more will just be more detailed bad news. Eliza will be able to help. I doubt she'd want to do anything else until she can't any longer. She understands my mother in a way I can't."

"That's okay, RJ," Julian said. "It's what she's trained in. Some people are good at understanding math and physics, others the ways and working of the human brain and body. You're not inept."

RJ snorted, hard. "Geez, how'd you do that?"

Julian smiled gently. "Nail you for blaming yourself for something you can't control? It's a talent."

Gregory studied him. "What do you do, Julian?"

"Pediatrics nurse." He answered without looking away from RJ.

"Ah, so you understand the human psyche as well." Charlie seemed impressed.

"Sometimes. I just prefer the pint-sized versions. They can't hit as hard when they punch."

RJ huffed and Charlie chuckled.

"The doctors seemed pretty sure she couldn't hit remission or last through treatment?" Gregory cupped his hands, tapping his chin.

"Not at this stage. Chemo has never really been an option because of the location of the inoperable tumor. They didn't know how it would react, and if it went negatively, it would have had a larger impact on her, likely killing her nearly outright. That's the cause behind her memory loss. Surgery was a last-ditch effort for one of the tumors, but that was only if she didn't have other cancer growths. The alcohol didn't help the speed but it would have come now or five or ten more years down the road."

Gregory slipped a hand under the table and Julian knew it was to hold hands when they shifted closer. "RJ. What would be best for you? Do you want us to stay, help take over some of the bills, stuff to help out, or do you want us to go and leave you alone?"

Julian waited as RJ straightened, never letting his touch slip from the man at his side.

"You'd do that? Help out?"

"Of course," Charlie was quick to add. "If we stayed, of course we'd pay our share. Groceries are nothing, really, and my accounts are in transfer, so money won't be a problem soon. We can help any way you need, especially after what you did for us." Charlie tipped toward Gregory and a glimmer in his gaze was quickly shared, then he faced them again.

"What did he do?" Julian knew there was a story behind that snuck glance.

"Helped me find Greg to apologize for being an ass." Charlie grinned. "Best friend ever." He winked to RJ, who chuckled, warmth adding color to his wan features.

"But is that what you want, RJ?" Gregory studied them both from across the table as RJ grew silent to think on it for a minute or two.

"If you two are comfortable here, I think it would help. Pamela can cover the office if I need her to. I'll warn her things are going to be in upheaval when I see her on Monday."

When RJ shifted to gaze at Julian, he told him, "Whatever you need, babe. I meant that from day one."

RJ's lashes lowered, hiding a hint of guilt, most likely at the way he'd treated Julian, but he was willing to forgive and forget.

"Thank you, all of you," RJ said. His features lost some of the drawn strain when he sat straight. "Okay, I need some happy. Tell me about the new position, Gregory."

"Well," he began, a devilish drawl in his words. "First, you both have to be naked."

"Greg!" Charlie growled at him.

"Just doing like he asked," he retorted with sheer innocence, a hand waved in RJ's direction.

"Not *that* kind of position. Your *research* position."

Gregory smiled broadly in answer to RJ. "Well, technically it is for research."

RJ buried his face in his hands, shaking his head back and forth. Julian felt RJ's shoulders relax under his palm and knew the banter was normal, smothering his smile with his drink. As the conversation shifted from RJ's mother and his looming problems, he relaxed more, his energy returning.

And not once did he ask Julian to stop touching or caressing him. Maybe he was making ground with the man after all.

CHAPTER ELEVEN

"THANK YOU, Dr. Lyttle." RJ hung up the phone, feeling numb. He set the phone on the table next to the couch, staring at nothing in the early morning of mid-April. Eight weeks had passed and the constant monitoring of RJ's mom had proved their prediction overly optimistic. She had been admitted to the hospital three days before and was on a respirator now, barely hanging on.

Samson came up and put his nose on a knee, staring at him with huge brown eyes. RJ petted him. "I know why Gregory picked you. I don't know anyone who could turn away from a face like that."

Samson wagged his tail, grunting in agreement as RJ scratched behind his ear. RJ stood from the couch. "Come on, outside time." Samson trotted over and waited obediently until RJ could get the door open for him. He let his forehead fall to the glass once it was closed behind the happy canine.

RJ had been busy with clearing his mother's house, securing her valuables, which really weren't many, and tying up loose ends. Thankfully, Grandma had the foresight to do a will and to make her daughter do one at the same time. RJ doubted his mother ever remembered doing it. Now she wouldn't remember anything.

Pamela had been all but running the office alone for the last two weeks as it was. RJ was just waiting for the phone call from the hospital. They all knew it was coming.

Straightening, with Samson outside playing and not ready to come in yet, he walked to his bedroom. In front of his dresser, he crouched to pull out a bottom drawer. Inside were a stack of pages and a couple files. Halfway down the stack, he found the file he needed.

He'd collected all his mother's legal documents weeks ago, including the original court documents for his child support.

Sitting on the floor, he leaned on the dresser and settled the pages and folders in his lap. Taking his time reading through them, he recognized some, and others were irrelevant. When he reached the paperwork on his father, he stopped.

In his mind, the man had absolutely no right to anything in their lives. RJ didn't want to contact him for himself. If he had, he would have done it long before now. No. RJ was doing it for his mother. The man had destroyed her, left her pregnant and alone, an adulterous mistake. RJ doubted the man had any good character qualities considering, but it seemed he should be told that Monica was dying.

Gripping the pages he needed, he dropped the rest on the floor, then stood, dusting off his Dockers. Walking to the small desk where his laptop sat, he opened it and booted it up. It only took a few more clicks to get to his e-mail. Immediately, messages popped up, and he felt just a small smile as he took them in, reading each one.

Julian sent him something daily from his phone. Sometimes it was a text or an image. If he couldn't, he e-mailed or called after work. RJ had come to look forward to these little treats from Julian, small moments when he could push away the ordeal of tying up his mother's life.

RJ knew he'd be handling all of this a whole lot worse if Julian hadn't been around. Gregory and Charlie had taken two weeks to go to LA. Gregory needed his background checked and police records done for the college, which took time, and unfortunately, none of the red tape went quickly or smoothly. They all hoped he'd be completed with processing by the end of the spring semester to start his new job first thing in the fall. Plus it gave them some alone time and a chance to play near the beach. RJ hoped, in truth aside from the reason, they had a wonderful time.

Focusing on what he planned to do, he steeled himself, then popped his knuckles. With a new screen opened, he typed in the e-mail address he had, a business account from the last court documents issued at the end of his support term. Maybe it would work, maybe if he was lucky, it would bounce and RJ could say he tried.

He only wrote a few short sentences.

Mr. Terzi,

My name is Randall John Sommers. You might recall my mother, Monica Sommers. I am writing only to inform you that she is dying. If you wish to make any last contact, I suggest you do so at your earliest opportunity.

RJ Sommers

Send.

A weight he hadn't been aware of shifted in his chest. Maybe he needed to do this, regardless of the reason. He leaned back in his chair to let his eyes sink closed. Considering he was basically sitting at home, pacing with a sick anticipation by the phone for the final call, he felt he was handling things rather well.

He stood and replaced the pages with the others, shutting the drawer, hiding it all away again. He stopped in the bathroom to piss, then reversed to let in Samson. His e-mail dinged as he crossed his bedroom threshold.

Expecting another little perk from Julian, he was utterly shocked to see his message had a reply.

Mr. Sommers,
Please call me as soon as you receive this.
Stefan Terzi

A phone number followed.

Holy fuck. His dad. RJ's legs shook as he sank to the bed a few paces away. Either he was going to chew his ass out for breaking the unwritten no-contact understanding, or he was honestly calling for Monica.

RJ doubted it was the latter.

Scribbling the number on a sticky note, he strode to the couch and picked up the phone in a clutched, shaking hand. His heart pounded like heavy feet were marching across his ribs. Steeling himself for the coming moments, he dialed the number.

"Stefan Terzi."

His mouth was dry. "Mr. Terzi, this is RJ Sommers."

Dead silence. *Great. He really hadn't expected me to call.*

He cleared his throat on the other end. "One minute please, could you?"

RJ rolled his eyes, but heard when he directed someone out of his office. *Right. Don't want anyone to know about your dirty little secret.* He moued scornfully as he waited, an arm going around his middle. He stared out the window, following as Samson loped back and forth chasing bugs.

"Forgive me," he said, a little brokenly. "But I have to ask this. Are you really Monica's son?"

"Oh, for fuck's sake," he griped. He threw his loose hand into the air, then wrapped it around his waist again. "Yes. I'd offer blood tests, but I didn't contact you for me. Monica is dying. I don't know if it matters to you or not, but this is your last chance to say goodbye to her."

"What happened?" he asked, calmer.

"She has cancer. Her prognosis was six months. It's down to weeks now."

"And this is the first anyone has thought to contact me?" His tone was cooler, leaning toward outraged. RJ reined in his own anger at the patronizing tone.

"We had strict instructions to never contact you, since you were already married when you screwed my mother."

"What are you talking about?"

"Look, I don't give a shit if you want to say I'm related to you or not. If you want to see Monica, this is it."

"No, you don't understand."

Rage began to filter through his control. "I understand perfectly. You have a legitimate family. Fan-fucking-tastic. I didn't call to get a father. I called to put my mother to rest."

"For Christ's sake, RJ, will you shut up! I'm trying to tell you I wasn't married. She was!"

"Oh, please! My mother was never married a day in her life. You can't come up with a better lie than that?"

"I'm not going to argue over the phone."

"Good," RJ retorted bitterly.

"Give me until tomorrow. I'll be there to see her and you."

"Whatever. Prepare yourself. She doesn't look anything like she did thirty years ago, and she was an alcoholic."

"Oh, God." Stefan's broken voice shuddered through the phone. "Where do I need to go?"

RJ gave him the hospital name and his phone numbers.

"I don't blame you for being angry—"

"I'm not."

"—but there are a few things that obviously need to be cleared."

"I only called for my mother, Mr. Terzi," he informed him coldly, his eyes narrowing as his emotions seethed. "Whatever you think will happen with me, won't."

"I'll talk to you tomorrow, RJ. And thank you for letting me know about Monica."

He forced some of his anger out of reach. He didn't know this man; he meant nothing to him. "You're welcome. Goodbye."

JULIAN KNOCKED, then opened the door. "Babe?"

"Kitchen."

Samson trotted up, sniffing his greeting along with RJ's called voice. "Hey, guy." He closed the door, then petted the lab. When he stood behind RJ, he wrapped his arms around a trim middle. "Any news?"

He closed the refrigerator, leaning into Julian's strength. "Dr. Lyttle called this morning. She's comfortable."

Julian laid a cheek to RJ's shoulder. He'd backed off trying to get too personal with RJ while he was dealing with his mother, the hospital and the doctors. Being a friend and supporting him when he needed it was more important than being physical, though he wouldn't deny he badly wanted the man in his arms. His need and desire hadn't diminished in the least.

"I also contacted my dad. He's coming tomorrow."

Julian gave a light squeeze. "That was a nice thing to do, babe."

A shrug moved the body in front of his.

"Maybe. I did it for my mom." RJ turned in his arms to settle his body into Julian's. "Thank you."

Julian nuzzled him in return. "What for?"

"For being here. For being a friend. For forgiving me for being an ass. I know I've been a shit the last few weeks."

With a supportive hand, he lifted RJ's chin. "Babe, you have good cause, and I understand that. I'd be a wreck in your shoes." Julian also knew he could forgive RJ just about anything.

"Would you stay tonight?"

Julian gazed into his earnest gray eyes. "Are you sure?"

"I'm tired and stretched, but you don't have to treat me with kid gloves. I know that's what you've been doing."

"I just didn't want to add to your stress, babe."

RJ's fingers danced upward, sliding through his hair. "Honestly, what I need is for you to hold me. After what I did..." RJ bit his lip. "After what I did to you, I didn't want to push, but I don't want to sleep alone tonight."

"With just anyone, or with me?"

"Don't be a dick," RJ groused. His forehead fell to a shoulder with a dull thud. "Yes, just you. Seriously, Samson is not my type."

Julian chuckled lightly. "Okay. Let's do something about dinner and relax for a while."

"That sounds marvelous," RJ replied, hugging Julian tighter.

RJ HONESTLY didn't care what they did, he just needed a few minutes of anything that wasn't hospital, mother, or father related. Stefan had called again barely an hour before Julian arrived letting RJ know the flight he would be on. He didn't have far to come, only from Phoenix. RJ was treating him like an ancient acquaintance of his mother's, and nothing more.

At least Pamela had done a good job at keeping fires to a minimum while he went through this. The woman was getting a summer bonus, no question.

He leaned against the counter as Julian made himself comfortable in the kitchen. The man wasn't shy about using anything on hand as he cut and sautéed, washed and chopped.

Gregory wasn't kidding. He had RJ beat hands down, too.

"How'd you learn to cook so well?"

"Me and Toni both learned from Mom. We helped out a lot in the kitchen. It was fun."

RJ rested on a hip, content to watch the man at work. "How is Toni?"

"Doing great. She and Leslie have a son now."

"Wow. I have really been out of touch." RJ shook his head. *That was only last spring, wasn't it?*

Julian rolled a shoulder, tearing lettuce leaves to toss in a bowl. "It wasn't a huge secret, but she was pregnant when they married. They beat the preacher."

RJ chuckled with a rueful undertone. "Been known to happen. Are you sure you don't want any help?"

"Nah. This is pretty simple to make. The definition of salad is if it's edible, toss it in a bowl." Julian glanced his way. "Would you like to learn? I've always wanted to take a cooking class. Learn a few new things." He smiled a little grin, those dimples coming out. "You probably don't know this, but I have a small addiction to the food and cooking channels." He held up his hand and pinched two fingers together. "Small," he repeated.

RJ liked watching him, following the humor and pleasure on his face. "Uh-huh. I can tell."

Julian picked up a pan off the stove with boiling eggs in it and began to run cold water over them to cool.

Next, he picked a handful of waiting grapes to toss in with the greens.

"Grapes? Really?"

"Wait until you get the flavor. A little burst of sweet." Julian plucked one. "Come here." He lured RJ forward with the enticing offering. "Open up."

RJ followed Julian as he neared, piercing, watchful eyes intent on him. The cool smoothness of the grape swept over his lips, painting them with a sweet pressure. The delicate skin of the grape was cool to the touch. His heart began to beat a little heavier, a little faster beneath that searing gaze. The fruit was placed gently between his lips, and he licked the offering finger with the tip of his tongue.

Julian zeroed in on RJ's mouth.

"How is it?" Julian asked, his voice huskier than a few minutes before.

He tasted the grape as it burst over his tongue. "Delicious." *But not as delicious as you.*

"RJ," he all but moaned. "Don't look at me like that."

"Like what?" he asked, leaning forward to bring them nearly body to body. Flat palms found their way to Julian's chest. The heat of skin scorched RJ.

"Like you want to skip dinner," Julian replied.

CHAPTER TWELVE

RJ INCHED his hands upward over Julian's still-smooth jaw. Skin burned his palms, desire sparking over nerves as he neared his goal. He couldn't explain his infatuation with Julian's ears, but he wanted to touch them, taste them, nibble on them.

Julian's hands settled to RJ's waist. "Are you sure, RJ? I can wait."

RJ paused his exploring. "Is that what you've been doing? Waiting for me?" He straightened enough to peer into Julian's expectant face.

"Mostly. It's been hectic for you, and I didn't want to see you just to have sex with you."

"I've barely had time for anything." RJ ran a fingertip over one of Julian's ears, noting the slight quiver of his body as he did so. RJ barely had time to shower, or so it seemed, since his mother's prognosis in early February.

He'd had to make sure he could handle the financial burden of his mother's last days, clear her home, prep the home for sale—he had no need for it—cancel her accounts. There wasn't a day he wasn't doing something as they all waited. He made it a point to visit the hospital as well. It did little to sit and stare at her, but he knew if their places had been reversed, he would have wanted at least some acknowledgement. He spent a lot of the time reading for her, something he knew Eliza had done regularly.

Julian's fingers tightened and loosened reflexively as RJ continued to outline the ear under his fingers.

"Exactly," Julian said, drawing out the sensations of fingertips to skin. "I've been waiting."

RJ stopped, gazing at the angel face before him. "That is the sweetest thing anyone has ever done for me or said to me."

When Julian closed the space between them, RJ didn't stop him. Warm lips ghosted over his. His pulse jumped and blood began to race. Fingers danced over his waist and he looped his arms over Julian's head, teasing hair with light flicks. Soft pants of air warmed his skin, made him ache. His heart fluttered, making him feel flushed all over.

Julian's tongue recreated the path he'd made with the grape, teasing over RJ's lips with the tip, and his eyelids closed as sensation bombarded him. RJ bowed, hungry for contact. Chest to chest, they stood in the kitchen with Julian short-circuiting RJ's mind.

Julian hummed in appreciation, then delved between RJ's lips, stroking his tongue, and RJ answered. Blood pooled south, his groin tightening as their bodies nudged and glanced against each other's.

The strength of a hand formed to his back as Julian aligned them, teasing RJ with the subtle grind of his cock. RJ shivered hard, his exploratory touch turning to grasping as need licked at him. Hunger burned hotter with each taste and thrust of Julian's kiss. They were both breathing heavier when he finally let RJ go.

"Sweet." Julian sipped another kiss. "You're making me forget about feeding you," he warned.

"Then I'm doing this right." RJ smiled, glancing through his lashes. "Dinner will hold."

A warm palm fitted to his jaw. "I'm not going to let you fuck and run again."

RJ shook his head. "We'll do it right this time."

A sound of longing rumbled from Julian, and he was kissing RJ again, passionately, stealing his last sane thought. As far as he was concerned, this was far more important than dinner.

The next time Julian let him go, they moved together to quickly place the salad and anything that wouldn't do well on the counter in the fridge. Then he was crushed into Julian's embrace once more. The counter edge pressed into his lower back when Julian turned them both to capture him with unmoving arms bracketing him on either side.

"Home alone, right?" Julian asked, sucking tender kisses up and down RJ's neck.

"Until Sunday." He tipped his head, hungrily welcoming the hot, seductive caresses.

"I love the way you dress, the way clothes just mold to you." Julian said as he nuzzled the hollow of RJ's throat to swing up and swipe the bob of his Adam's apple with a hot tongue. Deft fingers dipped beneath RJ's shirt, questing beneath fabric, then easing buttons loose. RJ felt as teeth and lips left behind drugging memories as Julian floated over his collarbone and neck, leaving behind little nibbles of pleasure.

The collar of his shirt fell over his shoulders to trap his arms close to his sides. Julian took blatant advantage, lapping and kissing bared skin. He murmured in appreciation, licking his lips to rake his teeth over the tightening bud of RJ's nipple.

RJ groaned, his head growing loose on his neck. He gripped the counter to stay on his feet, his knees feeling weaker by the minute.

Julian continued to unbutton RJ's shirt, tugging it out of his waist. Seeking lips trailed like brands over his skin, making him tremble with desire. Then he took long swipes over RJ's ribs, laving over them like he was a treat to enjoy.

He straightened, panting, to claim RJ's lips in a hard kiss.

"Love the way you taste," Julian rasped when he finally released his mouth.

Tremors rolled over RJ's shoulders, falling down his frame in waves of desire. RJ tugged the loose shirt free, then tore it off, tossing it to the counter. "You. Got to feel you," he moaned. God, he wanted to touch Julian. He was going insane with the need to feel him under his palms.

Julian didn't argue. With swift yanks, his shirt joined RJ's. Then RJ leaned into that hard chest and felt fire pour into his veins. He rolled his hips, trying to ease the tightness of his cock locked behind his zipper, teased awake by the tender kisses that started it all.

"Want you naked." Julian's voice raked over his senses with a hoarse vibration, his lips and teeth attacking the side of RJ's neck and shoulder.

His lips quivered. "Bedroom." It was a gasp that degenerated into a moan of pure pleasure when Julian latched onto his pulse and sucked. *"Uhn..."* He sighed, shivering when tingles shot like fireworks down his frame.

RJ's skin felt electric, shocks and heat careening wildly, making his heart beat faster, making his shaft throb harder, striving for relief.

Julian stood, dragging out every motion, every brushed caress. "Take me there."

It wasn't the voice that startled RJ. It was the request. Staring into twin hazel pools, he panted, swallowing with a noticeable gulp. Nodding, he acknowledged that he heard and that he understood. Julian wasn't going to let him run twice, and letting RJ lead the way made it his choice.

Patience softened Julian's face, his palm cupping his chin and caressing him. "I know, babe. I won't hurt you."

RJ shook. "You can't promise that."

"You have the same ability to hurt me, RJ, just as badly, just as deeply."

I do? Lashes fluttered to rest on his cheeks when Julian pressed a warm kiss to his lips. He realized in a flash just how much he had hurt him those months ago. His heart pounded, trying to climb upward. Julian's voice disrupted its journey.

"Take me to bed."

He shuddered. Stark hunger filled those words. RJ sighed in surrender and Julian let him go. Paving the way, he found one foot in front of the other, crossing the living room well aware Julian was behind him.

"Sexiest fucking walk," Julian murmured in his ear when they stopped next to the bed.

"That's why you wanted me to go first?"

Julian chuckled evilly. "One of the reasons."

RJ spun. Wrapping his arms around Julian, taking him unawares, he took them both off-balance to tumble to the bed. A tussle ensued with Julian's deepening laughter easing some of the tension raking through RJ.

He wanted Julian. It was the risk that was terrifying him. Julian stopped beneath him and RJ straddled his hips with his hands braced on his chest. "You're a devil in disguise," he accused. "Those dimples." Julian had the nerve to smile broader.

Strong palms formed to his ass, massaging, and RJ arched. He couldn't concentrate when Julian was doing that. "That's dirty pool."

"Just appreciating," Julian replied.

RJ moaned deep in his throat as fingers created magic wherever he touched. Claws dug into Julian reflexively, and he hissed low in response, his body trembling between RJ's straddled thighs.

To RJ, that was the sexiest thing he'd ever seen in another person. Pure abandon, unadulterated pleasure. He leaned forward and kissed Julian, letting their bodies rock against one another with Julian's hands guiding his hips as he rolled to grind down for friction.

Sleek muscles bunched and gave under him with Julian's motions. They pressed tighter and he shuddered, the scrape of skin and chest hair driving him deeper into a whirlpool of need.

The teasing trail of fingertips slid to the button of his Dockers. With a swiftness that RJ couldn't follow, Julian had them loose and his hands inside, cupping what he'd been holding just moments before from the outside of his pants.

"Oh, God," he cried, his lips just above Julian's.

"This is why I followed," he remarked with a husky purr. Julian muscled him down and devoured his mouth, thrusting between his lips. Fingernails scraped seductive patterns, then delved between to plunge through the valley with learning fingers. RJ gasped, then whimpered as he danced near, but never touched where he needed relief. Shivers rippled over him with each stroke. "Want you, baby," Julian growled, biting with light teeth to RJ's chin.

RJ tumbled from his perch above Julian, slipping off the side of the bed. Calming Julian's expression of worry and surprise, he let his pants fall off, his underwear shimmying down with them. A renewed desire ignited. With an arched eyebrow, he spun on a heel and hopped to the restroom, gathering what they'd need, supplies he hadn't touched since Toby's departure.

He placed the lube and condoms on the nightstand once he stood by the bed, gazing at the delicious god waiting for him.

Crawling onto the bed, he rested on his knees, quickly undoing Julian's jeans, the zipper sounding loud between the two of them. With a little cooperation, the offending garments were dragged down his legs and tossed to the side.

It didn't seem to matter how many times he saw Julian in the buff, he was knocked speechless by the sight. Not a perfect six-pack, but a solid man, a man with strong arms who loved to touch, be touched and so much more. Dimples, a chest worthy of worship and a mouth with a talent for pleasure. There was no secret to how much RJ liked his cock, the taste, the shape, the heat. He almost moaned, taking him all in, eating him up with his eyes. Julian made him feel like he'd won the lottery.

"Now who's staring?" Julian graveled, with a teasing grin.

"Missed you," RJ admitted, his voice raspy with need. When Julian lifted a hand, RJ sank willingly, stretching out along his length. Fingers danced over his face to thread into his hair. Lips warm and tender kissed his. RJ's pulse quickened. He pressed his groin into Julian's hip, shuddering as shocks rose from his balls to his brain. Then he was on his back, Julian staring at him, grinding down in hungry circles. RJ's brain disconnected as he was thrown into sensory overload.

"Julian," he panted. Suckled love bites were drowning him in shivers. His hands were pinned to the bed, all of him captured by Julian. His hips lifted, hungry for more. The slide of hard flesh against his cock made him tremble and stiffen at the same time. He felt dampness on his skin and craved to glide together harder, friction sending needle-sharp pricks cascading over his skin.

Julian moaned thickly, the sound hot beneath RJ's ear. "You feel so good. I love touching you." Julian maneuvered lower and RJ waited with anticipation. Julian hummed with a hungry need and RJ almost lurched at the flick of a tongue over the head of his shaft.

Released, his hands flew to grip at Julian's hair, his neck arched as he mewled for more. He cried out when he got it. Warm, wet heat enveloped the tip of his cock. Swirls of a teasing tongue made him shake.

When Julian opened up and took his cock deep between his lips, RJ shouted, his eyes popping open, yet unseeing. "Julian!" A strong arm weighted down his thighs, keeping him from thrusting into the cavern of pleasure swallowing him whole. "Aww, fuck, Julian." RJ rocked his head, his fingers clutching hair as though Julian was his only hope of keeping him on Earth.

RJ was panting raggedly when Julian lifted. "I want to taste you, but I want inside you so bad, baby."

He swallowed, unable to speak. His pulse pounded like a timpani against his ears. He tried to focus, his fingers falling limply from their clawed hold on him, amazed Julian never once complained, never pushed him away.

RJ would give him anything, would do anything so long as he didn't stop. Mustering a modicum of strength, he wandered fingers through the same strands he'd just held on to for dear life, caressing Julian's face and cheek. "Love me right," he said, knowing Julian would understand.

The spark that appeared in his hazy gaze proved RJ right.

CHAPTER THIRTEEN

RJ WHIMPERED. Julian's fingers touched him everywhere. Teased him. Tormented him. His tongue and lips followed. The bedding bunched under his hands when moist heat bathed his sac right before Julian lapped one full nut into his mouth. Julian's moan of pleasure was echoed by RJ's keening cry. Gasps shook the bed as he tried to remember which way was up, and then simply quit trying, riding the wave. The teasing tip of Julian's tongue roamed the skin beneath and between. Then Julian tossed a leg over his shoulder, splaying him like an offering, and took full advantage.

A rocket of feeling shot up his spine when that same tongue swirled over his pucker. He trembled from his shoulders to his ankles.

"Oh, oh, God." He gasped, thrashing to push against the pressure probing at his entrance.

"So hot, RJ," Julian murmured, barely heard. More damp, more tongue, then Julian's finger glided in. He swept the flat of his tongue over his balls. Slow and deep, Julian sawed in and out, teasing, tempting and driving him out of his mind. A drugging hard pull, sucking his marble-hard balls between taunting lips, had RJ grasping for his shaft, needing relief.

Julian released him. "No, babe. Not yet."

RJ whimpered. "Please. So good." He let his hand fall away when it was apparent Julian wasn't going to continue with anything unless he did.

He wanted to cry. He ached, his cock so hard with the need to come, drips leaked from the tip to land on his overheated skin. Julian licked them up, moaning.

"Julian. Please."

The sensation of questing fingers returned. This time they eased into his channel coated in slick. Julian curled his fingers and found his trigger.

"Oh! Fuck!"

RJ arched, striving to impale himself on those teasing digits, harder and deeper.

"Damn, babe. You're amazing."

RJ whimpered. Like he could talk? The tear of the condom packet sent a wave of goose bumps down his arms. Then Julian was above him, gliding his hard cock into RJ's channel with measured thrusts.

"Relax, babe. Fuck, you're tight." Growls filled the room.

"More! God, please, more," RJ begged on broken gasps.

Then Julian was seated, and they each drew a staggered breath. RJ trembled. Stuffed and feeling desperate for more, for him to move. Julian rocked his hips, friction shooting sparks and flames through RJ's body. Hovering above him, Julian sought RJ's lips and he met him, capturing his tongue and suckling on him, pulling him between his lips to the music of Julian's moaned pleasure. His hips rolled. RJ's hands whipped up and latched onto tight shoulders.

"So good," RJ managed, his heart pounding into his ribs. His cock throbbed as his balls hardened more. Each roll and thrust brought him closer, wound him tighter.

"RJ." Julian groaned and RJ wrapped his legs around his hips, grinding to meet each thrust.

"So close." RJ was panting, delirious.

A kiss, then Julian shifted to his knees, taking RJ with him, keeping his legs locked around his waist. "Want to see you come, baby. Want to see your face."

Julian moved again. RJ shouted as the angle ground the head of Julian's cock over that special place. Hard and deep, Julian filled him and RJ lost it.

With a silent scream he arched his back, clawing fingers driving him into the pleasure Julian delivered, jetting over his abdomen and his chest as he was swept under and drowned in heat. A heartbeat, two, and his voice filled the room, followed within seconds by Julian's raw shout of release.

Throbbing as he filled the condom, pressing even tighter against the sensitive walls of RJ's channel until, with a grunt and final jerk of his hips, Julian's fingers relaxed from where he'd clutched at RJ.

RJ's heart jerked and thundered, as though restarting with a kick. It just might have. It felt like he could've died, or had an out-of-body experience. He'd never felt anything that intense in his life; no one had ever made him that desperate. Cooling skin sent fresh tremors over his body as air caressed him in gentle drafts.

He was so spent, he wasn't sure he could even open his eyes.

A moan was dragged out of him when Julian slipped away, letting tense legs relax to the sides of his thighs. A moment later, he felt as Julian's weight dipped the bed, followed by a soft towel wiped over damp skin.

RJ felt utterly drained, completely melted.

"You're incredible," Julian praised him gently. When Julian was done, he stretched out with RJ, held on a palm to watch him from above. Fingers drifted in lazy patterns up and down his chest. "I think I'm addicted."

RJ tilted in his direction. "Oh?"

"You're so smooth. It drives me out of my mind. Touching you, tasting you." RJ watched as a lengthy shiver shook Julian. Just moments after the heights of their pleasure, Julian's dick twitched, tapping RJ's hip. "I want you to know, I haven't been with anyone since I met you, RJ. Even after you left me like you did." He caressed the side of his face with the feathery stroke of his fingertips. "I'm not a player."

RJ studied his features, sheer truth clear in his gaze. "I believe you," he said. "Is that your way of saying you want to make a go of this?"

Julian grinned, a rough snicker echoing behind his lips. "You could say that."

RJ captured his hand and brought it to his lips, brushing gentle kisses to the knuckles. His heart tripped as he considered his words. "Since Toby, there's only been you."

"Is that your way of saying yes?" Julian countered.

RJ returned his smile. "You could say that."

Julian brought RJ into his frame, wrapping him into his embrace, taking them both to the bed. "How 'bout a nap then that dinner we were working on?"

"I'd like that," RJ replied, snuggling in, content. He could take this a minute, a day at a time. Julian was a rock RJ needed in his life at the moment. He'd worry about later...later.

RJ SQUEEZED Julian's hand before he got out of the car outside one of the main entrances. He'd picked up RJ to not have to face the day alone. RJ hadn't even asked. He knew Julian was too good for him, and this proved it. "Thanks, Julian." The hospital loomed over them like an emotionless wall. White, with multiple windows, and as bland as flour.

"Anytime, babe. Is he here already?"

"Probably. Said he was going to check into his hotel, then come right over." RJ stared at the building, hesitant and unsure why.

"I'm just at the other end if you need me."

RJ faced Julian, the quiet offer in his words warming. "I know." He squeezed Julian's strong palm once more. "Don't worry about me."

Julian leaned across the console and touched lip to lip. The small gesture made RJ's heart flip.

"I'll see you in a few hours."

RJ nodded, letting him go and getting out. He watched Julian drive around the bend to park in the staff lot. Squaring his shoulders, he turned on a heel and went inside.

To visit his mother.

To meet the man who was his father. He was more than hesitant. He was nearly nauseous. Mercifully, Julian hadn't made a point of it when he'd said he'd already eaten, though RJ hadn't. He was just as sure Julian knew it too. He'd left in the early morning to shower and change, then returned to pick up RJ, support for the coming day. Julian was going to check on his kids, as he called them, giving RJ time and space, but was there if he needed Julian. Another reason Julian was too good for him. He'd done nothing but treated him like shit and the man was still there, willing to hold him up.

Shaking his head, lost in thought, he exited the elevator on his mother's floor. He checked at the nurses' station for an update, then walked on until he stopped at her open door.

A man he didn't know sat in a chair at her bedside.

Black hair, more curls than RJ's, with a similar build, though not really showing his age the way some couldn't avoid. A stylish polo in royal blue and dark slacks. He could have been a man in his forties—if RJ didn't already know exactly who he was.

"Mr. Terzi."

Stefan didn't raise his gaze. "You can call me Stefan, RJ. If nothing else, I can be a friend, of sorts."

RJ refrained from making a sound or comment, his hands slipping into his slacks pockets. The silence between them was filled with the pinging sounds of monitors, the whoosh of the respirator. He had no desire to fill it, either. She didn't look much different than she had four days ago, but she was. More gaunt, pale. Wasting away. They might not have been close as some could be, but she was

still his mother and watching her fade ate at
him.

"How long has she been like this?"

"She was admitted four days ago. She's not
in pain."

Stefan was holding one of her hands, his
thumb stroking the back absently. "That's good
to hear." A sigh filled the room. It sounded full
of regret, full of loss, and full of things best left
unsaid. Stefan wasn't the kind though. "There's
so much to tell you, least of which is I'm sorry."

RJ shrugged. He walked into the room,
shutting the door for privacy. He leaned against
it. His heart was beating hollowly, still waiting
for the shoe to fall, for whatever would happen,
to happen.

"You really didn't know she was married
before?"

"You don't have to lie, Stefan."

He arched an eyebrow. "I have no reason
to lie. It was a range of events. If you don't
believe me, check her records."

"I have them all."

"I mean the public records. Her husband's
death will be in the city obituaries."

RJ frowned, staring at the man who still
hadn't looked at him too closely, trying to cut
away the lies from the truth.

A heavy weight seemed to settle over
Stefan when he quietly asked, "Tell me
something, RJ. When did your mother start to
drink?"

"I'm not really sure, before I was in school.
It didn't turn into an addiction problem until
I was about seven." He was pretty sure that was
when his grandmother started to visit more, or
something...

RJ was surprised to see Stefan's desert-tanned skin blanch. "I had no idea. She pushed me away so hard." Stefan's eyes were filled with pain, remorse and guilt when he finally looked in RJ's direction. "Why don't you sit? This isn't the best of circumstances for what I need to tell you, and having you watching me like you're expecting me to sprout hydra heads is unsettling."

"Hydra heads?"

"Sorry. I'm a fantasy buff. Love the Greek and Roman mythos."

Unsure of what to do with that, RJ did as asked and pulled the second chair in the room closer. Stefan turned to face him, though still maintained contact with Monica. RJ guessed he was rambling, as unsettled as he himself was. At least they were on equal footing with that.

Stefan's gaze fell inward and he began. "I cared for Monica, but learned I didn't, couldn't love her. She was married, though it was brief. I met her during one of my family's vacations. What we shared was very whirlwind. When we both realized it wasn't meant to be for us, she fell into another relationship and was married within four months. She shared with me one secret, that she was already pregnant, and made me swear I would never contact her or you."

RJ pinched his lips. "All very accommodating. Grandma swore the exact opposite. You were married, had an affair with my mother, and refused to acknowledge us."

Stefan's gaze hit him square. "If I had done any such thing, I never would have offered the child support when I learned her husband had died in an auto accident."

RJ leaned forward with his elbows on his knees. "You offered?"

"In an instant. RJ, I've never been married, well, not in the sense most expect."

He'd spotted the ring, though Stefan didn't make any efforts to hide it. Censure was clear. "Common-law marriage is upheld in almost every state. Nice try."

Stefan's gaze swept away, intent on still holding his mother's hand. He was obviously trying to decide his next words, weighing them. "She made me stay away, RJ, though if I'd known how it all would have affected her—"

"Stefan, stop." He stood to stiff legs from the chair. "You're not doing yourself any favors. We all have regrets and wishes to change things. I told you coming here wouldn't be for me."

A tap on the door preceded it opening a crack. "Stefan? Oh, I'm sorry. I didn't know RJ had arrived." He went to close the door, but Stefan halted him.

"It's okay, David. Come in. This might help clear up a few things."

David did as asked, his hand on the handle of the room door, cautiously watching them both.

"RJ, this is why your mother and I couldn't marry, and why your grandmother, most likely, didn't want you having contact with me. RJ, David. My husband."

RJ's mouth fell slack.

He blindly reached for the chair, falling into it. With a glance, he spied the gold band on David's hand, assuming when he'd arrived the ring's mate Stefan wore would be on a woman's hand.

Stefan continued with his story as if there had been no interruptions.

"After your mother, before her husband's death, I met David. She did try to contact me, which was how I found out about her husband's death, and she learned about David. When she and her mother learned about us, they made me verbally agree to never contact you. I fear it was learning about me that caused your mother to turn to alcohol," he brokenly whispered, regret tingeing every word. "Then, except for the money being sent to her, I never heard from her again beyond what the state sent me in updates."

RJ's chest burned as he tried to find air to breathe.

"I know it's probably a disgusting shock to learn your father is gay, but there it is."

RJ barked a laugh, then scraped a hand down his face. "Oh, fuck," he gasped. He stumbled from the chair. "I need some air." David leaped out of the way as he hurtled for the door, then tore through it.

He almost ran, though didn't, conscious of where he was, just to get outside. The automatic doors flew open as though anticipating his rush, his tangled emotions clawing through him as he put distance between himself and the men in the room. He marched around the grounds outside, his mind whirling, his heart pounding until he could think nearly normally. Finding a bench, he sank down to it, his face held in his hands.

RJ had never questioned his grandmother, and his mother had never spoken of either man. If it weren't for the story he'd known growing up, he might as well have been an immaculate conception.

A part of him believed Stefan, actually wanted to, and could see his arguments vividly, but thirty-three years of knowing differently couldn't be dissuaded that easily.

Gregory could help him track down the truth. He understood records and how to find the needle in the haystack. If she had been married, there would be a trail. It wouldn't take but a little time to find out who was telling the truth.

Kneading his scalp under tight fingers, he didn't notice right away when someone sat next to him.

"Could you give him a chance to just not hate him?" David asked quietly.

"I don't hate him." RJ wasn't sure how he felt about Stefan.

"We both knew about you," he said. "Though there's no excuse for staying away for so long."

"That's a moot point now. You're here."

David agreed with a tilt of his head. "Honestly, I'd always feared your resurgence."

"You have?" RJ peered toward the fit blond. Also desert-sun tanned, with clear blue eyes behind thin rims of steel.

"Monica was the only thing in his life he'd ever truly regretted." When RJ stiffened, he rushed on. "Not because he got her pregnant, but because he couldn't include either of you in his life. Not even as a friend. Whether it was intentional or not, regardless of who it came from, he was cut out of your life, and hers. I know he did like her. I think it was a combination of that summer and myself that was the turning point in his life. It took him almost two years to come out of the closet."

"Why are you telling me this?"

"Because I doubt he told you how it affected him, just the facts." He smiled ruefully. "That's Stefan. He goes through life with this façade that nothing hurts him, that he's impervious. So he only shares the superficial details. Especially with you."

"What's that supposed to mean?"

"It's why I always feared your appearance. You're the only person who has the power to take him away from me."

RJ rolled his eyes. "Gawd."

"I don't think you understand, RJ. If you walked into that room right now and told him you could be his friend, try to be a son, he'd do it." He snapped his fingers. "Like that. Regrets will do that to a person. Make them react. Discovering her like this, knowing it could have all been avoided, changed, lessened, whatever... He's been dying in chunks since yesterday."

"Please," he scoffed.

"I'm telling you this, RJ, not to make you pity him, or to mock him, but because behind it all, he's got a huge heart. It's one of the biggest things I love about him. I'm sorry you're disappointed that he's gay, but I won't let you hurt him more than what he's already doing to himself."

"Fuck, David. I don't care that he's gay."

David looked at him square. "You don't?"

"No. It explains a shitload, though."

"Your sense of fashion?" David tried to tease.

He snorted. "No. The fact that my boyfriend's name is Julian."

David's mouth formed a round oh, his eyes widening.

"Grandma died before I realized it, and Mother hasn't been well enough in almost a decade for it to matter."

David sat shoulder to shoulder on the bench, leaning forward the same as RJ.

"I'm not telling you how to treat Stefan, though I hope it will be with respect if for nothing else, as another person, and a past friend of your mother's. Just bear in mind, there's a part of him that's always been open and ready for you. Tread on that spot carefully."

"Is that a threat?" RJ twisted to stare point blank at the man at his side, trying to read the meaning behind his words.

David didn't evade him, meeting his stare with unblinking eyes. "No, just a request from the man who loves him like he's my whole world."

CHAPTER FOURTEEN

"HOW LONG are you two planning on staying?" RJ asked David as they walked back into the hospital a little later.

"A couple days. We'll go home, but can be here in a moment's notice."

RJ opened the door for them. "I'm sure she'd be happy if she knew."

"Thank you, RJ." When he gave David a questioning glance, he said, "For not spurning him, for giving him even this. What happens, happens."

"Give me time, David."

"That's all any of us can do," he replied wisely. They made the remainder of the walk in silence.

His phone buzzed a few feet from his mother's door. David nodded and let him have some privacy, joining Stefan in the room. He pulled the phone from his pocket, and felt a small tingle of happiness seeing the number.

"Thought you weren't allowed to talk on the floor," RJ said in greeting.

"I'm outside the ward, and technically on break. How are you?"

RJ backed up a few paces and leaned against a wall, wallowing in the concern in his voice without guilt. "It could have been a lot worse."

"Is he an axe murderer?"

RJ chuckled, knowing he'd made that assumption once or twice during discussions over their pending meeting. "There's a few things that took me by surprise."

"Oh? Good things?"

RJ slipped a hand into his slacks pocket, resting against the wall. "Maybe just things that I can understand. Though I do plan on making sure he's telling the truth. I need to talk to Gregory when he gets home."

"It'll work out, RJ. Everything happens for a reason."

RJ shook his head, hearing the same sentiment from Julian that he'd just heard from David.

"Why do you put up with me?" RJ mused, focusing on the man on the phone rather than the heartache waiting for him.

"Because you moan cute?" Julian said with a teasing air. "Come down here when you need a break. There's someone I want you to meet."

"To the kid's wing?" His shoulder twitched. "Julian, I told you..."

"Get over yourself, RJ. You're being paranoid."

Was he? RJ *was* dealing with a lot of stress. "Okay. I need to call Pamela too."

"See you in a bit. Got to go."

"Bye, babe." RJ didn't want to let him hang up; he needed Julian's smooth voice and calm to keep him from jumping to conclusions and seeing things where there weren't any.

Checking in with Pamela only took a few minutes, his schedule being managed by her capable hands. He was going in for a while on Monday. He'd spent some time there during the week, but knew he couldn't ask or expect

Pamela to do the work for both. It did no one any good to be at the hospital nonstop, anyway.

He entered his mother's room finding David behind Stefan's shoulder. Stefan stood, placing her unmoving hand on the bed. "We're going to get lunch."

"All right. You're welcome to come and go as you please."

"RJ?" Stefan neared to stop in front of him. "I wouldn't blame you if you said no, but would you give me, us, the chance to get to know you?"

RJ wanted to step out of the room, let them leave, and not have to answer. He owed them nothing, yet when he couldn't find the words to keep him at arm's length, he nodded instead. The grateful relief in Stefan's eyes—nearly identical gray to his own—made his chest hurt.

"Don't take it as an insult, RJ, but you are the image of your father when he was your age." David slipped a hand through the crook of Stefan's arm. "Come on, love. You need a break," he whispered for Stefan.

"The waiting is the worst," Stefan managed, his voice thick, RJ forgotten. "Just like Mama."

"I know, babe," David crooned. He gave RJ a parting glance, then led Stefan away.

RJ watched them leave, wondering if it was Monica or memories that were weighing him down. Maybe it was those regrets David had mentioned. He didn't know.

RJ could do nothing about any of it.

Before leaving the room, he studied his mother lying on her bed, unaware of the tumult she was causing with the only man that he'd ever known existed in her life. Feeling a tightness in his chest, he realized he wasn't as distanced, as apathetic as he'd believed. If there'd been a chasm between them, he'd helped put it there. His mother wouldn't have known to do it. She wouldn't have known to hate him, spurn him or love him. He left before the swarm of emotions took over and toppled him.

INVESTIGATING UPWARD from where he laid stretched on the play mats across the room from the entry, Julian spotted RJ leaning on a shoulder against the wall. With a flickering smile on his lips as he took in the scene, Julian suddenly felt himself blush, not quite embarrassed but unprepared for the warmth of having him near. And getting busted playing with the G.I. Joe green army men.

"That explains oh, so much," RJ teased, grinning with a secret wickedness meant only for Julian.

Three pint-sized bodies whirled. When the three did, Johnny turned to see as well.

"Who are you?" Marlo asked.

"This is RJ. A friend of mine." His heart sped up, feeling the heat in those gray eyes. The man's gaze smoldered. Tearing away, he brought himself under control.

He lifted a hand over each head, introducing them. "This is Tiffany, Marlo, Garret and cute stuff here is Johnny." He tapped Johnny on the shoulder and hand-signed for him. He smiled and nodded vigorously.

"You know sign language?"

"I'm certified to teach it. I've been helping Johnny here." He laughed when Johnny pointed at himself and spelled his name. Julian tapped his little nose, making him giggle. "Who is also already too good at lip reading."

Snagging on RJ, he noticed he'd focused on the children, the emotions clear on his face, realizing just why he was in the recovery ward. He stood straight from the wall. Julian waited for him to say his goodbye and run, expected it, really.

"This is why you volunteer?" RJ asked with solemnity.

"Part of it." He didn't want to come out and say it was also because Tiffany had no family to help her, visit her. Julian didn't dote on her any more than the others, but he wouldn't stop helping her either. "Where is Stefan?"

RJ rubbed a hand over the nape of his neck. "Went to get lunch. He had someone with him."

Julian had expected as much. Though RJ's next words blew his mind.

"Um, a significant other. David."

Julian sat up completely from his lounging position.

"Are we going to play more, Julian?"

He snapped out of his daze, focusing on Marlo. "Sorry, yes, but give me a minute. Okay?"

He hopped up and closed the distance between himself and RJ. "Seriously?"

"I know. I didn't think my day could get any weirder." RJ slipped his hands into his pockets. At that moment, he looked so lost, so unsure. He'd just met his dad, only to learn he was gay. Wild.

Julian made a fist, wanting to touch him, to curl him into his arms and give him what he needed, at the least to let him know he wasn't alone.

He couldn't.

RJ cleared his throat. "I didn't mean to take you away," he said, motioning with a twitch of his chin.

Looking behind him, four sets of eyes were glued to him.

He returned to RJ. "Want to play army men?"

RJ swallowed. "Will me being here get you in trouble?"

"Do you have a criminal record?" he asked, joking and grinning to show it.

"Yeah, I'm wanted in all fifty states for being a sap."

"Then you're fine. Come on."

With RJ at his shoulder, he reclaimed his place on the mats to the side of the room, sitting cross-legged. It tickled him when RJ did the same, uncaring that he'd be resting on the ass of his dress pants. "Do you guys mind if RJ plays with us?"

The boys shook their heads, with Johnny following their lead, his eyes huge as he took in RJ. Tiffany was looking at the floor, picking at the hem of her nightgown.

"So, show me what we're playing," he offered.

Julian shared a smile with him, appreciating RJ giving the kids the control. He began to wonder if what he felt was something stronger, something deeper.

RJ didn't make one gesture or one comment about any of the scars, healing burns or Marlo's damaged leg.

In that instant, if he could have, he would have pounced RJ to the floor to kiss him breathless.

Instead, he dumped out more molded plastic figures from the container at his side until they littered the mats between himself, RJ and the kids.

For thirty minutes, the boys made explosions and toppled major cities. The whole while, Julian snuck glances to Tiffany. She didn't leave, but she didn't play either. Julian bit at his lip, trying to think of a way to help her to open up.

She was used to Julian. It wasn't healthy for her to close up around others. He had a feeling the insults she'd been getting from Garret's brother had done more damage than just hurt her feelings.

A knee nudge drew his attention to RJ. He rolled his eyes toward Tiffany, a question in them. RJ was aware. Flipping through ideas in his brain, Julian was coming up empty. She usually wasn't that quiet.

RJ leaned close, his hand cupping his mouth to whisper faintly, "Nail polish?"

"That's okay, but I don't have any."

RJ's eyes gleamed. "Be right back." Julian watched him stand and walk out of sight.

Johnny waved to ask if he was coming back. Julian smiled, motioning yes. RJ had an admirer.

RJ's lean legs brought him into the room about fifteen minutes later. "Eliza left it in Mother's room." A bottle of coppery red nail polish was in his hand. He held it between his fingers. "But Mom doesn't need her nails done. I wonder if there's any girls who would like to get their nails painted."

Tiffany twitched, her gaze lifting to shoot to Julian.

RJ sat next to Julian again, his gaze light and open. "What do you say, Tiffany? Girls don't want to play *just* army men, do they?"

Tiffany shivered, then shook her head stiffly.

"Well, let's see those piggies. We got to make them colorful." RJ flipped out a hand, waggling fingers, using a flamboyant tone to emphasize each exaggerated motion.

Tiffany's shoulders trembled, then she giggled.

Julian watched him in awe. RJ was a natural, enticing Tiffany out of her shell. Within minutes, he was lightly holding her fingers, making her laugh in peals of joyous sound. He could only shake his head when two nurses stopped by the ward doors, curiosity apparent in their expressions.

"Not me," Julian mouthed when they stared at him, then at RJ, who was practically nose to nose with Tiffany as they chattered while he painted fingernails and toenails.

The nurses left, shaking their heads in amazement.

Julian knew just how they felt.

Following the pair on the floor out of the corner of his eye, a warmth suffused him from the inside out. With her blonde head and the raven-haired brunette, side by side plotting world domination, he realized something.

He was falling for RJ.

But something even bigger was there, gazing at the two of them together. He needed both of them to make him complete.

CHAPTER FIFTEEN

RJ WAS WALKING through his front door not a full two weeks later when his cell phone rang. He recognized a number from the hospital. The caller didn't matter. The order was to call this number when...

"Hello?"

He closed the door quietly, Samson wagging his tail in greeting.

"Mr. Sommers? This is Dr. Huggins at Mercy Memorial. Your mother has passed away."

He swallowed the lump in his throat. "Thank you. I'll see the rest is put in motion."

"My condolences."

He murmured another near-silent thank you, pressing the button that would end the call. His hand was shaking as he dropped it to his side, the phone clutched but forgotten. With his eyes closed to stem the pressure, he saw nothing surrounding him.

"RJ? Is that you?" Charlie called out from his shared bedroom.

He swallowed, fighting to sound normal. He failed. "Yeah."

Charlie walked into the room in shorts, his knee brace and nothing else. "You all right?"

Working his throat, he shook his head.

"Oh, man." Charlie neared and hugged RJ. "I'm sorry, man."

He welcomed the warmth, letting out a shaky sob, embracing Charlie shamelessly. "It's okay. She wasn't in pain. That is better than most who reach the point she did."

"Do you want me to call anyone?"

Nodding brokenly, he handed over the cell. "Julian and Stefan, please. I need a few minutes."

Charlie cupped the back of RJ's head and held him tight. "Anything you need."

He nodded numbly and slipped away, closing his bedroom door behind him. He fell across his bed, gripping his pillow against his chest, and tried to breathe. He could, but only through the tears.

JULIAN TREATED RJ with a light touch over the next week or so, by his side for the funeral, for every minute RJ needed him. Though by the end of a month, when RJ was still listless, he began to worry. He understood grieving. He understood regrets, and knew RJ was neck-deep in them.

After another week passed and RJ was still mired, drowning deep in whatever pool he'd thrown himself into, Julian decided drastic measures were called for.

When he knocked at RJ's front door and Charlie let him in, shaking his head, Julian frowned. He knew from Gregory that the story Stefan had shared hadn't been make-believe. Everything RJ had known growing up from an infant to less than two months before had been a lie, fabricated, then unchangeable, because the only people who could tell the truth weren't around to do so.

Even if RJ wasn't as receptive, Stefan, David and Julian had formed a friendship, with all of them worried over RJ's state of mind. Even Tiffany, after only one afternoon, had asked for him, and that had almost broken Julian's heart to tell her he didn't know when RJ would be back to visit.

Steeling himself, he knocked on RJ's bedroom door and then opened it. "Babe?" Julian found him balled up on the bed. "Okay, this has to stop, RJ." He sat on the edge of the bed. "You have a business, friends, a house to pay for. You can't keep this up."

"Go 'way," he grumbled, not even looking in his direction.

Julian stood from the bed and grabbed RJ by the ankles, yanking him with a squeal of surprise to the edge.

He snarled, glaring at Julian. "Leave me alone!"

Julian got in his face. "You've had your 'poor me' party. Time to wake up and get your ass back in the game."

RJ shoved himself away, scooting across the bed. The sweats he wore twisted as he tried to flee. Julian grabbed them in tight fists and let him disrobe himself.

"What the fuck!" He reached for them as they slid down his hips and thighs, but Julian was quicker, whipping them off lean legs before RJ knew what Julian had planned.

"You're getting in the God damned shower if I have to carry you over my shoulder!" He braced himself on his knuckles to meet RJ's glare head-on. "Pamela is running RJS Events *by herself*. You're a fucking prick to leave her alone like that. Your friends are worried about you. The man who could be a friend, or even a father if you'd let him, is worried about you." His voice evened. "RJ, I'm worried about you. And you want to know what killed me? Having to tell Tiffany I had no fucking clue when you'd be back. I've never heard her laugh like she did for you. You don't even know her story and you didn't care. What's sadder is you still don't."

RJ crossed his arms. "You can't."

"Don't tempt me, sweetheart," Julian growled. "I've never been violent, but you've made me mad enough. This makes the second time."

"Don't forget us!" Gregory's voice echoed through the door and Julian snickered.

"RJ, just let us help you. You are outnumbered."

RJ flopped down to the bed again, fisting the sheets. As if that would be enough to deter Julian and his strength would be greater. Julian had hit his limit and nothing was going to stop him.

Julian felt RJ would break, let whatever it was he was holding inside out if he pushed hard enough. Luckily for everyone, Julian had the patience, strength and balls to deal with a scrabbling Greek with a penchant for using elbows and knees. He knew Gregory and Charlie were up to their eyeballs trying to figure it out to no avail.

That left Julian.

He leaped, pinning RJ to the bed, who screamed in a caterwaul that echoed through the house. He wrestled off RJ's shirt, oomphing when he was caught in the ribs by an elbow. Captured beneath his broader frame, he held RJ's wrists together.

It took some maneuvering, but he rolled him to his stomach and shackled his hands low behind his back. "Now stand up, darling. Time to hit the showers."

"Fuck you!"

"Not until you're cleaner," he answered, dead serious. Panting, he tugged a jerking and fighting RJ off the bed and pointed him towards the bathroom. "Gregory!" The door popped open. "I can't let him go to start the water. Could you, please?"

He was halfway across the room when he asked, "Hot or cold?"

RJ glared murder at all of them. "Bastards! Get your shit and get out!"

"Normal—no. Cold. He needs some shock therapy first." Julian toed out of his own shoes as he spoke. His clothes could get wet.

"Fuckers!"

Gregory looked right at them as he exited, the sound of the water running clear while pain streaked over his features. "You going to be okay?"

"Eventually. He might scream some more, but I'd never hurt him."

RJ wrenched to get free. Julian didn't let him slip an inch. "What do you think you're doing, you ape?"

"Let's go, sexy." He thought he heard the bedroom door close, but didn't really care. RJ was tiring but still fighting him every step of the way.

He didn't pause inside the bathroom, just wrapped his arms around the other man and with him pinned to his chest, stepped over the tub wall and under the freezing stream. The scream that ensued probably reached the pearly gates, but he didn't let go, shoving as much of a nearly naked RJ under the spray as he could. He still wore his briefs.

Harsh pants flexed his body as he struggled against Julian and against the chill of the water. RJ gradually went limp in his arms, his head sagging forward. Water splattered all over, hitting them both and beyond, but he didn't care. The man in his arms was his entire focus.

As minutes passed, he loosened the grip he had on RJ's wrists, feeling him flex his fingers in response, though not yanking them away from Julian. He stroked the soft skin of RJ's inner wrist, his forehead settled to RJ's shoulder as every ounce of stiff energy drained away.

Almost as suddenly as the fight began, it ended, a soul-shattering sob the only sound between them. When RJ wavered, exhausted from putting up a fight, Julian wrapped his arms around his middle and let the storm break. Sobs and wounded moans echoed in the bathroom as his entire frame shook with the force of it.

"That's it baby, let it out," he crooned.

RJ leaned forward, pounding the tile as he choked out howls and whimpers of pain, until even those began to dry up. Julian didn't know how long it took, only that he held him and refused to let go. Weakly, RJ turned around in increments and wrapped his arms around Julian's waist, shivering.

Julian reached and adjusted the water spray. "Better?" he asked tenderly.

RJ nodded, his head a dripping lump on Julian's shoulder.

"It's okay, babe. It'll be okay." With patient hands, he bathed RJ, slipping drenched underwear down to shove into a corner of the tub.

Julian scrubbed every inch, even taking the time to wash his hair, relishing the feel of the black silk. It had been weeks since he'd made love to RJ. Touching him, holding him, soothed Julian as much as it soothed RJ's pain and trembles.

"That's it, baby. Let it go," he crooned when a shuddering moan escaped while Julian worked fingertips over RJ's scalp.

Groggy, he opened weary eyes to stare into Julian's. "You know, you're still a bastard."

A half smile curled Julian's lips as he rinsed out RJ's hair. "Yeah, but I'm a sexy bastard."

The first glimmer of humor that Julian, if not anyone, had seen in RJ since his mother's passing sparked in his gaze. Relief made him feel light.

"What was it, babe?" he asked, massaging his back and neck as the water warmed chilled skin. Julian didn't push, letting RJ find the words, letting him reach the end of the road he'd put himself on. One Julian hoped he was ready to leave.

"Guilt. For not trying to help her sooner, for taking their word as gospel and not trying to find him. For so many things."

"Shh." He brushed a light kiss to RJ's damp forehead. Julian understood, though they both knew his mother's condition wasn't treatable, even in the beginning. As for Stefan... "You have him now, if you want what he's offering."

"I don't know yet," RJ admitted, his embrace tightening around Julian. "Hey! You're still dressed." Big gray eyes opened wider. "You did this while dressed?"

"Whatever it took, babe. This is a very small sacrifice." He brought RJ's mouth to his own and warmed himself with a kiss. He turned off the water, then reached for a towel. "I am getting pretty good at doing this for you," he remarked with a drawled tone.

"Let's get those off of you and in the dryer. Gregory might have something that would fit you."

"Are you sure? You just kicked them out."

RJ's expression morphed, appalled. "Oh, crap. I did, didn't I?" He yanked the towel out of Julian's hand. He motioned to Julian, hurriedly swiping over his body with the towel. "Take those off. I need to go talk to him. Shit. I'm an idiot."

"Hey. Baby. Relax. I'm sure he's still here." Julian tried to calm his frantic motions.

"Yeah, but I was still an ass." He popped up and quickly stole a kiss. "Julian?"

He paused undoing his belt and snagged on RJ's guileless orbs. Shadows remained, but it was a start. "Yeah?"

"Thank you."

I love you. His heart hit his ribs as he swallowed what he craved to say. "You're welcome," came out instead. He sighed, trembling in the aftermath now that RJ was out of the tub and racing around the bedroom jumping into clean clothes.

He sank to the edge of the tub to work himself out of his sopping jeans, feeling like he could use a good cry himself.

CHAPTER SIXTEEN

JULIAN GOT OUT of the tub to find a pair of jogging shorts on the bed and a T-shirt. Donning those, he held his soaked clothes in a ball, carrying them with him from the bedroom.

A shirtless Charlie reached for them. "I'll toss them in. They're out on the patio." Charlie motioned over his shoulder and Julian spotted RJ and Gregory sitting at the deck set, earnestly in discussion. He didn't want to intrude on that.

"Okay. Thanks."

When Charlie walked to the garage, Julian was instantly drawn to the scars on his back. "Hey, Charlie?" Julian followed, wanting to ask, yet hoping he wasn't overstepping their friendship.

"Hm?" He shut the dryer door and hit buttons.

"You don't have to answer, but how did you get hurt?"

Charlie didn't look up, his focus far away with his hand splayed on the dryer. "I was burned. A house fire." Julian realized he'd never seen Charlie in shorts, and RJ had said something at some point about a brace.

"I want to ask you a favor," Julian said quietly. "You don't have to, but I think someone I know could really benefit from talking to you."

Charlie looked up finally.

"One of the kids I visit at the hospital." He told Charlie about Tiffany, the accident, being

146

alone, and being scared and scarred. "She's only seven and we both know it's only a matter of time before they turn her over to adoption services. She's terrified that she's too damaged to be loved again." The child advocacy people were trying to find her family members but weren't uncovering any in the woodwork.

Charlie leaned his hip on the dryer, crossing his arms to study Julian. "What can I do?"

"Show her that it doesn't change the person she is."

Charlie's face grew solemn. "It does, though, you know."

Julian's heart thudded heavily, knowing he wasn't asking a small thing of the other man. "I know it does, but not in the way she's imagining. It doesn't help that one of the other kids has a brother who's an ass and insults her every time they visit."

"Seriously?" His eyes widened in dismayed shock.

"Yeah." Julian sighed, raking a hand over his head. "The father cuts them all down and the brother copies him. I love the kids, but I'd also love to teach dear dad a thing or two from my point of view."

"From Mr. Knuckles' point of view?" Charlie asked, grinning.

"Exactly." Julian plowed on. "You don't have to, Charlie. I know it's got to be tough sharing what happened. I volunteer in the recovery ward of the pediatrics wing. Tiffany means a lot to me," he finished quietly.

Charlie crossed his arms and studied Julian, and he was sure his request would be denied.

Waiting for the man to decline, he was shocked when he heard, "If Greg can go with me, I'll do it."

"Really? I mean, I'll take everyone and have a party."

"Nah." Charlie chuckled, letting his arms drop as he straightened. "He drives better than I do. Can't get used to this California craziness."

"You will, man." Julian glimpsed over a shoulder through the doorway to zero in on the two on the patio. Both were smiling and laughing. What he found warmed his heart. "That right there is worth everything today," he murmured. Charlie peered around him to see.

"Wow. That's a damned miracle." Charlie pushed on Julian's shoulder to get him moving. "Come on. They're having way too much fun."

Julian let himself be pushed around, unable to stop staring at the vibrant man sitting in the sun.

"Better wipe your face," Charlie warned. "He catches you staring at him like that, and the jig is up."

"What do you mean?" Julian was torn between losing himself in RJ's glow and trying to figure out what Charlie was yapping about.

Charlie walked around a stunned-to-a-stop Julian. "Julian, the only one who doesn't know you're in love with him is RJ."

RJ HELD THE phone in a sweaty palm. Each ring echoed in his ear. Stars sparkled overhead where he sat outside on the patio, his feet propped on a matched set chair. He tipped his head to let it rest on the cushion top behind him.

His heart pinched when the line was answered.

"Hello?"

"Hi, David. Is Stefan home?"

"RJ?"

He sighed roughly. "Yeah." RJ knew he made David nervous. He wasn't sure how not to. Only time would really make it clear, for all of them.

"Hello, Stefan," he said when the other man was there.

"How are you?"

RJ let his eyes drift closed. The concern in that one question, just three little words, was unsettling. "I'm doing better. I wanted to say thank you, for what you did, for being here, for helping. I haven't been in the best place in my own head recently."

"And now?"

"Let's just say I had a chilly awakening."

Stefan chuckled. "Julian?"

RJ's lips twisted with a hint of wry humor. The bastard had left about an hour earlier, but not before he managed to kiss RJ senseless. Gregory and Charlie were inside watching TV, which left him a little quiet time to do this. He curved his arm over his stomach, cupping his middle. "Yeah. Look, I know we can't fix what's been, and I'm not sure what I can give, but it's only fair that we try."

"Fair to whom?"

RJ tapped his ribs with loose fingers. "I guess you, and me," he replied, subdued. "I'm not looking for a father figure. Kind of grown past that, but I think I would like to get to know you."

"I'd like that too," Stefan returned. "In fact, why don't you and Julian come and stay for a few days? We have plenty of room."

"Are you sure?" RJ gnawed on his lower lip between scraping teeth. It was only an olive branch of friendship. He calmed the increased pounding of his heart with effort.

"Positive. Just pick a weekend."

"All right. I'll let you know."

"Fabulous. And RJ? Thank you for giving me a chance."

RJ swallowed the lump in his throat praying silently he wasn't going to regret reaching out.

"ARE YOU SURE you won't get in trouble with all of us with you?" RJ asked Julian. They walked side by side with Charlie and Gregory a couple paces behind.

"It's not a closed part of the hospital, and the kids are patients, like any others, allowed visitors."

"That sounds like you're circumventing the system somehow," Gregory said with a rueful hint as they strolled down the hallway, well-known murals of characters and landscapes reaching floor to ceiling.

"The only difference is I'm here on a Saturday." Julian would have crossed his fingers if he'd thought it would help. It was odd that they were all there to see Tiffany, but he wasn't telling a lie. Any of the kids could have visitors. Except with them being non-family, he could get in trouble. Probably would, but Tiffany was worth it.

"Julian!" Marlo spotted him first, hobbling over to leap for him.

"Hi, tiger. What's shakin'?" He caught him and hefted him into a hug, to place him on his feet again.

Marlo giggled. "Whatcha doin' here on a Saturday?"

"I brought some friends of mine to play, and one of them wanted to talk to you guys."

"Really?" Garret had run over too, Johnny right behind.

"RJ!" A female squeal that would have made dogs wince bounced off the walls as Tiffany came tearing from the play mats.

He blushed and chuckled, breaking into a full laugh as she grabbed him around the middle.

"Hey, button," he greeted her warmly.

"Why button?" Julian was amazed again at how she reacted to RJ. He didn't even have it in him to be jealous. Not if seeing RJ made her that happy.

"Because RJ says I'm as cute as a button." She said this with brisk punctuation, her head bobbing.

RJ shrugged sheepishly, his lips twitching to hold in his laughter.

"What's the ruckus in here?" a rumbled, not-too-strict female voice called just before she rounded the corner.

Julian cut her off before she could really get a good head of steam going. "Hi, Betty. We came to play with the kids."

She took one look at the four men, and her lips pinched. She narrowed her eyes and he almost cringed.

"Julian, can I have a word with you?"

"Uh, sure." He looked to RJ for some help. "Could you take them to the mats and play army for a few?"

"Sure." RJ smiled for the boys and Tiffany. "Who's ready for a battle of the boys?"

Pandemonium ensued as he led them to the mats, Gregory and Charlie trailing, though watching him pensively.

"It'll be all right. Be right there." At least he hoped it would be all right. He watched as RJ led the group to the other side of the room, like the Pied Piper weaving his spell. How the man thought he wasn't good parenting material, Julian had no idea.

He approached Betty and she crossed her arms. "It's not going to be a problem. Remember the burn survivor I told you about?"

She nodded, though watchful of the gaggle across the room.

"That's him. Well, the blonder of the two. RJ was the one who painted her nails."

Betty's gaze landed on each of the adults as they discussed their participation with the kids. "That's RJ? She hasn't stopped talking about him."

"Please don't put it down as an infraction," he said. "We're here to play, and Charlie will talk a little. That's all."

Betty sighed in a suffering way. "If Ms. Johnston finds out, I know nothing."

"Deal." He grinned, almost dancing on his toes.

"And don't let them out of the ward. Johnny's been sneaking to the nurses' station, and since he doesn't talk, we don't know he's there."

"He can't hear either," he reminded her.

"Yeah, but the stinker can lip read like he's been doing it for years," she whispered.

Julian covered his mouth to not bust out in laughter. "Okay, I'll talk to him. He might just want to go to his room," he offered.

"Nope, he's there being nosy. I've asked him plenty of times and he just smiles and runs back here."

"I wish his family would come visit more. He misses them."

"I'll make a note for their next visit to encourage them. It might help."

"Okay, so we're not going to be bounced out, right?" Julian asked, ready to get to the laughter and explosions behind him. Yes, he was guilty. He was a big kid at heart too.

"No, go have a good Saturday. I'm sure they'll love it."

"Thanks," he said sincerely, whirling to go join in the fun.

He plopped down next to RJ and Johnny immediately crawled into his lap. "Okay. We're here on the sly, but Betty is cool."

"I knew you were doing something," Gregory grumbled, though not with any heat in it.

Julian shrugged. Johnny tugged on his shirt and asked him why he was there. He communicated it while speaking for the others. "These are my friends, Charlie and Gregory—"

"And RJ!" Tiffany piped up.

Julian chuckled. "Yes, and RJ. We wanted to come spend a little time with you guys, and Charlie has something he wanted to share."

"You do?" Garret asked, sizing him up.

Charlie flushed. "Nothing like being put on the spot, man," he groused, shooting a dirty look to Julian. "But it's for the kids, so I'm letting it slide."

"And greatly appreciated," he replied instantly.

Julian signed for Johnny when Charlie began his story.

CHAPTER SEVENTEEN

RJ LISTENED as Charlie spoke, hearing it for the first time, but in a form that wouldn't traumatize the kids.

"Do you guys know what a fireman is?" Heads nodded in unanimous exclamation. "Great. Well, I was a fireman, and about two years ago, I was trapped in a burning house."

Four sets of children's eyes were glued to him. They weren't alone.

"Weren't you in your clothes?" Marlo asked.

"You mean my gear?" Charlie smiled gently at him. "No, this fire was at my own home. Someone started the fire with me inside."

Tiffany gasped and when RJ looked at her, she met his gaze and almost like magnets, snuggled up against him. He lifted his arm, unsure. She took the initiative and fit herself into his side. Knowing Julian was watching everything, he wrapped her closer, his arm around her waist as she listened.

"How'd you get out?" Julian asked, speaking for Johnny, who was making adamant motions with his hands.

"I was rescued by other firefighters. The reason Julian asked me to come tell you about what happened to me was because I was also scarred."

"You were?" Tiffany asked on an enraptured note.

"Badly. I know you can't see it, but..." He stretched out his right leg and flattened his jeans, exposing the outline of a linear brace that stretched from below his knee to halfway up his thigh. "This is a brace I wear every day so I can walk without a cane. I used one for over a year before I began to wear the brace."

Charlie craned his head to search the outer doors of the ward. "We're clear?"

"Yeah." RJ wondered why he was asking, then watched as Charlie tugged his shirt out of his jeans waist. "Walk behind me. It's easier at this point than me trying to get up and down on my leg. You'll see what I'm talking about."

With his T-shirt lifted to about mid-torso, exposing his lower back, one by one the kids crawled around to stare. Johnny's eyes got huge, his hand trembling as he lifted to touch the back of his head. Hair had started to grow again to cover his scars, but he'd always have the physical marks, just like Charlie.

The kids were speechless. Not that RJ could blame them. He'd seen Charlie's scars. It was a miracle he'd lived and all four of the men knew it.

Julian waved them to sit in a circle, like a group campfire. The kids did it without argument.

"I think the reason Julian asked me to come show you was because this just happened to me, and I lived. I'm still living. I'm about to start college in the fall—"

"You're not a fireman anymore?" Tiffany asked, reclaiming her close spot by RJ's side.

"No, I can't be. To do that, you have to be able to lift a lot of weight. I can't, but I'm okay with that. I'm happy; I have friends, people who love me. I even have a dog that I take for walks." RJ saw Gregory's grin at that. They walked Samson almost every evening for alone time. "It's different, it's not bad," Charlie added, then tucked his gripped shirt into his jeans again.

"What are you going to do?" Marlo picked up a soldier in his hand, turning it upside down.

"I think I'm going to do something with computers, programming or maybe repair. I have a few things to consider."

"Do people make fun of you?"

RJ glanced down, hearing the brittle uncertainty in Tiffany's young voice.

"Honestly, I don't know. It doesn't matter to me, though. It took a while to learn to ignore the feeling that everyone was looking at me. But know what I learned?"

Tiffany stretched to hear.

"Once I stopped concentrating on other people and more on myself, the idea of what other people saw or thought didn't bother me any longer. The feeling went away and I'm happier for it being gone."

"I remember those days," Gregory murmured tenderly. "Those sweaters."

"How do I make it not hurt?"

"Button," RJ said in answer. "That's part of focusing on you first. You have to make yourself happy. Others will try to hurt you, if you let them. If you don't let them, they have no power."

"Julian said the same thing," she said, chewing on her lip.

"There's a lot of things people will try to hurt each other over, Tiffany." RJ chucked her under the chin to get her to look at him. "Stupid things, like straight hair over curly, tall over short." *Being gay.* He held his tongue on that one.

"So if I don't care about the scars, they can't make it hurt?"

"Exactly. It's like not caring that you have amazing powder blue eyes and I have gray." He leaned close. "I *always* wanted blue eyes. Never got 'em."

She giggled.

A tug on RJ's shirt brought his attention to Johnny. "He's asking if he can have hair like yours."

RJ chuckled, tapping him on the nose like he'd seen Julian do a dozen times. "Some day." The smile he got from Johnny made him feel lightheaded.

"Dad!" Garret leaped to his feet and launched himself at his dad. A quick hug and he was placed on his feet. His mom gave him a longer hug.

RJ felt Tiffany stiffen at his side. "Remember, button. They're no more important than your elbows."

She peered at him, gauging him. "Right." Then she sat up straight next to him. "I wish you were my dad." She tugged on her nightshirt. "You and Julian. You could be uncles, right?"

RJ coughed, unprepared for that kind of statement to then be captured by the wide-eyed stare sitting across from him. "Uh..." He didn't know how to answer her.

"I've never had a dad," she said, picking at the hem of her gown. "Mama never talked about him."

His heart pinched. Clearing his throat, he told her, "I didn't have one either. I was raised by my grandmother." Technically he was; the deeper details weren't needed.

"How about a juice break?" Julian offered, nudging Johnny off his lap to stand. Johnny and Marlo cheered, all about the juice. "I need a stretch."

"Good save," Gregory said once all the tots were a few feet away, headed for the refreshment counter.

"I'm constantly surprised at how open she is with you, RJ. She's never once spoken about her mother since she's been here."

"Where is she?" Julian had never said.

Julian looked over his shoulder, then squatted. "She died before Christmas. The auto accident that scarred Tiffany."

RJ's stomach lurched. And here he was trying to tell her the scars didn't matter. She had much larger problems to deal with than any scars. He popped up to his feet, ignoring the blood tingles in his calves. "I told you I'm not good with kids. Trying to tell her all this stuff."

"RJ, you're amazing with her," Charlie pointed out, using the offered hand from Gregory to stand. "With all of them. I think you're not giving yourself enough credit."

RJ shook his head. They had it wrong. He wasn't good for kids, he had no idea how to deal with them. He'd spent too much of his childhood raising himself, he wouldn't have any idea what a normal childhood looked like now.

"Are you ready?" RJ went to walk around them all, to get as far as he could before he said something else.

He tried to avoid Julian's reaching hand. "RJ, wait—"

The sound of a sneered voice, if not the words, reached them both at the same time. As one they turned to focus on Garret's brother towering over a trembling Tiffany. Garret and his parents were across the room looking at an art picture he'd drawn.

"I don't care, Brody."

He leaned and whispered something, which was probably how he always managed to harass her under the radar. RJ watched her little hands turn into fists and she opened her eyes, landing on him and Julian.

Pivoting on a foot, she turned away from Brody and walked up to them. "They don't matter," she said emphatically.

"No one will like you," Brody shot at her retreating back.

"Well, that's a lie," Julian said clearly, frowning at the kid's brass.

He was maybe twelve and being completely ignored by either parent. When it became apparent Tiffany wasn't going to rise to the bait, her spine stiff, Brody blew out a scornful sound and marched back to his parents.

Julian waited beside RJ for Tiffany to calm down. It took RJ off his guard when she walked and stood right between them, her thin shoulders heaving as she fought inside against the torment of the older kid.

"I want to go home," she whimpered.

RJ ran.

"I'M SORRY, Julian." Ms. Johnston dared to look apologetic. Julian had his doubts there was any sincerity in it. She saw children come and go regularly; so did he. Some stayed longer, some only a few days. Tiffany had been in recovery since before Christmas.

"She's healthy enough. There hasn't been any family located and we need the space."

"What about her counseling?" Julian was grasping at straws. He knew if he was being told at all it was because the wheels had already been set in motion. Ms. Johnston had just given him an update on all the children he volunteered with. Johnny was staying for further tests to see if surgery may help his damaged inner ears, Marlo was going to therapy to rehabilitate his leg and Garret was going home. If he was needed, he'd have a new child to fill the gaps until he had four again.

"She'll still have access to it, and all the help she needs."

"But she's going into foster care," he said bitterly.

"I'm afraid so."

The news ripped his heart out of his chest. "Can I still see her?" Julian knew the answer, even though he was compelled to ask.

"You know you can't," she replied, in her typical no-nonsense demeanor.

He wanted to get far away from the front of her desk, find some dark, quiet corner and curl up, just him and his misery. "So I only have today?" The weekend before had been amazing, Tiffany and Johnny both being so open, and RJ...the man amazed him. It was all crashing around him today.

Ms. Johnston nodded dispassionately. "She'll be processed on Monday."

He swallowed. "Thank you, Ms. Johnston. I better get to the ward." He flexed to stand from the chair, her next warning making him pause with a hand to the back of it.

"Julian, if you can't remain impartial, you may need to take a break from your volunteer hours. We can't have emotional attachments occurring with every child you help rehabilitate."

"It's not every child," he explained. "After almost five years, I think I know how to remain distant. Tiffany is special."

He didn't look her way when she barely sighed. "She doesn't have family. A lot of children don't. You feel you're filling a need. It's natural, but not acceptable for your position."

Julian raised his eyes and didn't flinch. "Ms. Johnston, I know a lot of adults today that didn't have the support and love of family. The scars she has on her shoulder are only a fraction of what she'll endure during her lifetime if you put her in foster care."

"I'm sorry, Julian. I can't stop it."

He clenched his jaw from saying more. It wouldn't do him any good and it would only validate her assumption that he was unfit to volunteer. He turned away and left her office, walking the halls blindly.

They couldn't take her away, but he couldn't stop them either. She'd go into the system, an older child, wounded and insecure. He didn't know when it had happened, when she'd wound herself so tightly around his heart.

He'd always believed he'd be a father, loved children too much to not want to give his heart and soul to one, or maybe more. He was realistic and knew adoption was the sanest route, but a gay man? Alone? He still lived in a bachelor's apartment, the same one he'd been in since he'd upgraded out of nursing school.

He felt her slipping away from him and he couldn't think of one way to stop it. Quelling the rising heartache, he plastered on a smile. It wasn't his place to inform them of the pending changes. He just had to deal with the aftermath.

CHAPTER EIGHTEEN

THAT AFTERNOON, he knocked at RJ's and waited. "Come in!" echoed through the front door. Samson, the perpetual greeter, bounded across the living room to meet him. He patted the lab's thrusting head, closing the door behind him. Gusting laughter flowed through the house from the backyard. The scent of cooking burgers made his stomach gurgle. His stomach could eat even if he didn't feel like it.

He was still sick over the day's news.

"Hey, you going to just stand there, or are you joining your friends in low places tonight?"

Julian blinked, dragged out of his thoughts, realizing he hadn't moved any farther than where he'd stopped just inside the door.

"Hi, Charlie."

Then RJ walked out of his room and Julian straightened. "What the hell happened?" RJ flinched and Julian immediately wanted to take the outburst back.

"Nothing," came the toneless reply.

Julian marched up to him and tenderly palmed his cheek. The bottom half of RJ's face looked like a macabre rainbow. He was afraid to touch him, afraid he'd hurt RJ more. "Who hit you?"

RJ pushed him away. "It's nothing. I had a fight with Toby."

"Please tell me he looks worse," Julian said.

"I wish I could." RJ's voice was a whisper. He still hadn't looked Julian in the eye.

"What happened?" When it didn't appear he was going to answer, he grasped a hand and led him into the bedroom. He smacked the door shut. "Damn it, RJ. Talk to me."

He spread his hands, giving a dismissive shrug of his shoulders. "There's not much to tell. He came here. Said Josiah kicked him out and he needed a place to stay. I told him no, we argued and he hit me."

"Baby." He tucked RJ into his shoulder. "Is there a chance he'll come back?"

"I don't know." RJ sounded so tired to Julian. Gradually, he relaxed with arms winding around Julian's middle, nuzzling into his neck. "I was worried you'd think I asked him back if he was still here when you got here."

"Did you?"

"Fuck, no!"

"Then I don't think that at all."

RJ grumbled. "How was your day? Better than mine, I hope."

"Maybe worse." Julian ran fingers up into RJ's hair, caressing his nape. "They're processing Tiffany on Monday. She's going into foster care."

"I'm sorry, Julian."

"I know. Me, too." He tipped RJ up to get a good look at his face. "If he ever shows up while I'm here, let me answer the door."

"You're here less than two days total every week."

Julian rubbed his thumb up and down the top of RJ's spine. "We could change that," he said quietly. He really didn't want to leave RJ alone with a violent ex out there. He knew the man in front of him was his future, if he could just convince RJ of that.

"Are you saying you want to move in with me?"

"If you'll have me," he replied honestly.

RJ tried to pull free, but Julian kept him from completely escaping. "I don't know, Julian. Toby isn't a threat, he was just mad."

"Yeah, and what happens if he comes back even more pissed? What if he does more than slug you?"

"He wouldn't," RJ denied.

"Babe, before today, did you think he'd ever strike you?"

Gray eyes shot wide. "No," he whispered. "But moving in? Gregory and Charlie are here."

"They weren't today, and once school starts they're both going to be gone a lot." RJ still didn't seem convinced. Julian spun them until he could sit on the edge of the bed, tugging RJ gently down beside him. "Okay. Let me put it this way. I was going to ask you sooner or later, but I wouldn't ask you to move in with me at the apartment."

"Ask me what?"

Julian counted to keep himself from rushing. A beat for every knuckle he caressed.

"If you'd like to do the shacking up thing. Taking it to the next level." *One, two, three, four.* He followed the rollercoaster motion of his thumb on RJ's hand. "I think we could make this work. Really make it work, RJ."

"Like permanently?"

"Eventually," Julian answered. "RJ." *God, give me strength.* He had to be prepared in case this blew up in his face. He lifted and focused on incredible dove gray eyes. "I love you."

RJ FELT LIKE he was gaping, staring into an angel's face that could even tempt the devil. "Julian, I—"

Julian cut him off with a kiss.

When he released him, RJ followed him a fraction, then stopped. "Not fair," he accused, frowning at the man next to him. Julian could do that too easily, make him forget everything around him for a kiss.

"Don't say no yet. Think about it, at least."

"But we want different things, and I suck at relationships."

"Really? It doesn't feel like it to me." Julian tilted his head to study RJ, his gaze roving over his features. "This is a relationship, isn't it? I just said I love you," he intoned quietly. "I mean that. We're here for each other. And lucky for you, I think your friends rock."

RJ straightened to study Julian. He couldn't say it. Just hearing it stunned him. He cared, he knew he did, but love? It left him feeling too raw, so he completely avoided it. "What about your friends? Your family? Your plans for the future? Kids?" RJ squeaked on the last.

"Nice try. You know Toni, and my parents are going to love you. They might even remember you from Toni's wedding." RJ waited as Julian paused, his focus falling to their held hands. Thankfully, he didn't push for an emotional return. "Yes, I want kids, but I don't want to talk about that right now." He shuddered, the agony still too fresh for him by the flash of pain on his face. "Tiffany doesn't know she's leaving on Monday. Today was my last day to spend with her."

Needing to ease the pain for Julian, RJ raised his hand and stroked his jaw. "She really is a sweet girl. I had fun on Saturday with her."

Julian peered at him through his lashes. "Then why did you leave like you did?"

RJ's heart pounded. He should have known Julian would go right for the jugular. "Because I'm not father material. I don't know one thing about kids, much less girls." He didn't want to hurt her, and he knew it was inevitable. Her want to go home, to have a home, for himself or Julian to be her dad...it was too much. RJ couldn't deal with it.

"You're wrong," Julian argued. "I was watching you with her. You'd make a fantastic father."

"Julian, this is what I was talking about, different th—" Julian's lips found his, a little more forcefully than the last time.

RJ's raised hand curled naturally over his jaw and he clutched the hand holding his at the same time when Julian dipped with his tongue, testing for access. RJ moaned in his throat, a faint sound of need. His eyes closed with a flutter, falling into the stark desire of the kiss.

They were both panting a little harder when Julian released him. He pressed his forehead to RJ's, the light sweep of fingertips tingling when he caressed RJ's jaw, opposite of where Toby had left his mark. "One thing at a time. I want to be here with you, for you. Are you ready for that much?"

RJ bit his bottom lip. He wanted to ask what would happen when Julian was done with him, when he didn't want to be with RJ, when he didn't love him any longer, but was terrified of the answer. He'd have to pick himself up again and he knew this time it would hurt a whole lot more than it ever had with Toby. RJ didn't want it to end soon, but he needed to be prepared because it would happen. Their wants didn't mesh. RJ couldn't see himself with children, and Julian deserved to be surrounded by them. Except he did want Julian. He liked being with him. Julian had stood by him in a way no one outside of his closest friends ever had.

Knowing it was doomed to fail, knowing he should push Julian away, he found himself nodding in answer regardless, feeling sucked in by his gaze.

"You won't regret it," Julian whispered, ghosting teasing kisses over his forehead and cheeks. "Come on," he said, standing to tug RJ to his feet with him. Julian was examining his face again. "Did you put anything on that?"

"Something frozen from the freezer."

"Okay."

"It doesn't hurt that much. I think it looks worse than it actually is."

Julian seemed to consider that. "If you say so. Let's go eat. Gregory's making burgers?"

RJ let him take the lead when Julian slipped an arm around his waist, guiding him from the bedroom. His mind was whirling. When he was close to Julian, in his arms, everything seemed so much better, like he could do anything, and even more with Julian there. It was only when he wasn't, when RJ was alone in the dark hours of the night, that he began to doubt his decisions. Toby had lived with him and had left. Today, he'd tried to force himself back into RJ's life and he'd paid for denying him.

How long would it take for Julian to realize RJ couldn't travel the same road with him? Would he leave then? How long did he have before Julian began to have the itch to be a father? Would he resent RJ for holding him back?

It didn't take a rocket scientist to reach the conclusion that Tiffany being pushed into the adoption wheel was killing him. RJ watched Julian put his heart into every child he worked with. The man's capacity to do that amazed RJ. Again, he had to wonder just what it was he saw in RJ.

He slowed before they reached the gathering on the patio. Josh and Laurence had come to enjoy the evening with Gregory, Charlie and himself, Julian now a part of that madness.

When RJ halted, Julian did the same, waiting at his shoulder. "Did you mean it?"

Julian tilted his head, his knowing gaze roaming over every inch of RJ's face. "The 'I love you' part?" he asked in return, subdued. RJ nodded, trembling and unsure why. "With every part of me."

"But—"

Julian silenced him with a butterfly kiss to his lips. "Shh. I have patience, babe. I waited a year to know you. I can give you time."

For some reason, it still felt to RJ that time was his enemy, and he didn't know why. Julian's assurance that RJ could or would feel the same unsettled him. He was so sure, so

confident, and lately that was everything RJ
wasn't.

CHAPTER NINETEEN

EARLY ON A Friday evening a few weeks later, RJ knocked on the front door of the fresh-looking home. It looked like it had been built in the last year, it was so pristine. Large barrel cacti edged the front of the home, not excessive but enough to break the pea-gravel landscape. A narrow serpentine border of flowers grew to the opposite side from the front steps to the corner of the home, bordered in stacked, flat rock. It stood out in colorful contrast to the small area of lush green between the house and the roadside. A painted, ornate wrought iron fence, the same pale gray as the home with dark blue accents, circled the front of the home and along the sides to the privacy fence.

RJ was having a hell of a time wrapping his head around two men living in, much less needing, a two-story, three-car garage home. And if he wasn't too wrong, they had a pool. From what he could see of other backyards, which wasn't much with the high fences, many had them. Even the smallest house in the subdivision put his condo to shame.

He hadn't been raised in poverty, but this...this made his skin chill and it was nearly a hundred degrees outside. It was clear Stefan and David were in a league well above himself.

When a BMW sports coupe drove by, he shivered, feeling utterly out of his element. "I can't do this." He spun, his only intent to get away.

Julian's hands on his shoulders kept him from turning and running for his own car.

"Yes, you can. You're already here."

Just then, the lock on the inside of the door grated, with it opening next. RJ stood face to face with his father, with his stomach somewhere around his ankles.

"Hi! Come in. Come in." Stefan stepped clear and motioned for RJ and Julian to enter.

"Thanks for the invitation, Stefan," Julian said, offering to shake his hand.

"You made excellent time."

RJ heard distantly as Julian made small talk with Stefan. RJ wanted to fall into his lover's shadow and stay there. Tiled floors caused a scuff of steps as they walked, following Stefan deeper into their home.

"Something to drink?"

RJ blinked when a nudge in his ribs made him squirm. "I'm sorry. What did you ask?"

Stefan smiled indulgently, leaning on the kitchen island next to his partner, who'd waited for them. "Just if you'd like a drink. David makes a wonderful mango smoothie."

"That sounds good." RJ studied them both when David began to flit around the kitchen. "Can I ask something?"

"Of course," Stefan replied.

"How long have you been together?"

David reached into the refrigerator, then the cabinets, gathering ingredients. "Well, I was twenty-two, Stefan..." He glanced over his shoulder. "Twenty-four, right?"

"You know it better than I do," Stefan groused good-naturedly. He looked toward RJ and Julian. "Showoff over there knew he was gay, even if being out was still an impossibility for the most part." Stefan crossed his arms, a warm gaze traveling over his partner. "Meeting him changed everything for me."

David shook his head with mild laughter floating around him. "I know." He put a hand to his cheek. "That *heathen*."

"Mama forgave you." Stefan guffawed. "Anyway. I guess, carrying the one and being fifty-eight, that makes it thirty-four years now."

David wagged a finger. "Not all smooth sailing, but worth every minute." He dumped fruit into a blender, bustling around to fill a container with ice from the refrigerator door spout.

"So you really did meet right after Mom," RJ said. He wasn't sure if he should feel disappointed or relieved, maybe a little of both.

"The whole summer of that year happened within weeks between myself, Monica, and then David. I didn't know then how it would all play out, and I'm sorry, but I knew I couldn't love her. Not the way she deserved. She was already with someone else when she admitted to being pregnant with you. I didn't push the issue because she felt secure in her future."

RJ didn't balk when Julian curled an arm around his waist, welcoming his warmth and comfort, absorbing it like a sponge.

"I understand. She couldn't have known. Her husband, Jacen, died within two years of their marriage. I was still a baby." Hard to imagine, but it was true. So much happening when he hadn't even been out of diapers yet. He shuddered a little at the thought.

Stefan nodded, growing thoughtful. "That sounds about right. You were almost three when she came to me, and by then..." He lifted out of his thoughts and David gave him a soft smile layered with understanding. "We were committed." Stefan's head shook stiffly and he grumbled, continuing, "That went over about as well as could be expected. Initially, her mother didn't even want me to pay the child support, to have nothing to tie you back to me, but I convinced Monica in the long run, it was the best thing for you." Sorrow darkened his gray eyes. "I had no idea they would tell you that story though. It's no wonder it took so long for us to meet. Between them telling you that and Monica pushing me away with her mother's insistence, this may have never happened."

David approached and touched his cheek with the back of his hand. "It's okay, love. Forward, remember?"

Stefan's posture relaxed. "Thank you."

"You really wanted to meet me?"

Stefan met his searching unflinchingly. "I've always wanted to, yes."

RJ glanced to David, remembering what he'd said that day at the hospital. His mother and grandmother had definitely had a strong hand in keeping them apart. The sound of the blender broke the quiet. A moment later, David offered filled tumblers.

"Let's go sit on the patio," David said.

"Have Timber and Georgie settled down?" Stefan asked as they reached the rear door.

"They're fine now."

"Who are they?" RJ asked.

"Our two greyhounds. We're strong advocates for the greyhound rescue and when needed, we foster for the program. Timber is an ex-racer who is calm enough to help transition racing retirees into being a pet, and Georgie is our clown." David led the way to the back of the house. "They get excited when we have visitors and two at once can be a little overwhelming, so we let them calm some before siccing them on strangers."

RJ took a sip of his drink, feeling the smooth freeze of the ice and tang of the fruit on his tongue. Okay, David did know what he was doing with a blender.

He had also guessed right as he walked into the backyard. A huge rock-edged pool took up about a third of the yard, with a splashing fountain at one end adding a certain sound appeal. It helped explain the sun-bronzed tan of both men and the healthy physique they both carried. A broad expanse of green was edged along the fence with more gravel for lower water consumption, making the thirsty portion of the yard considerably smaller, though looking at it, he couldn't see a shortcoming to the design. The landscaping made the home still feel like a part of the environment, rather than a sore thumb dropped into the middle of it.

Almost as soon as he stepped foot on the stone patio, he was accosted by two cold noses.

"Timber, Georgie, back," Stefan said calmly, not even raising his voice. "Sit." They sat like statues.

"Wow. Wouldn't Gregory be jealous to see that?"

Julian chuckled. "I know. Samson isn't nearly that well-behaved."

At the curious looks, RJ said, "My roommate has a yellow lab. Good dog, still young, barely a year and a half old."

David nodded, claiming a chair. "We work with these two, and working with them keeps their training fresh so they're not nervous about things. Them being calm helps new animals during transition." Tongues lolled as they panted, almost in unison.

"Makes sense," Julian agreed. He looked up, hopeful. "Can we pet them?"

"Of course," Stefan said with a smile. "Call them and let them scent you."

RJ watched as Julian did, the pleasure on his face making him glow as the two graceful animals warmed up to him. He loved seeing that smile on his lover's face. It hadn't been there in at least two weeks. It made him ache knowing why.

"They're beautiful," RJ said, doing the same as Julian to befriend the dogs. One was a sleek black, the other a dapple gray. "Let me guess. Georgie is the black."

"You'd be right." Stefan leaned to relax into his chair. "So tell me what you two do, how long you've been together. You said roommate, too."

RJ relaxed as much as he could, playing give and take as they learned about one another. Julian answered too, though he was smitten by the dogs and it was clear Georgie thought Julian was the cat's meow the way he kept putting his head on a thigh and looking up with the hugest, dark brown expressive eyes RJ had ever seen. He couldn't recall ever being that close to greyhounds before and honestly could see why Stefan adored them. Graceful, with fine lines and sharp contours, they had a certain elegance to them. And the two Stefan owned were true gentlemen.

David stood a little later when there was a break in the conversation. "Let me go start dinner."

RJ glanced at his watch, surprised at how much time they'd spent talking. The dogs were resting in the shade on the cooled stone and the sun had moved to cast deep shadows.

Julian glanced in David's direction. "Would you like some help?"

"Sure," David answered.

"Sweet! I was hoping you'd let me play in that kitchen." Julian grinned like a kid.

David cast a playfully pensive look at RJ. "He does know his way around, right?"

"Most definitely." RJ was happy to brag about Julian. The man deserved it. Julian trailed after David already asking questions before the door had even shut, leaving Stefan and RJ alone at the table.

"He's a hell of a catch," Stefan remarked.

"Julian has been..." What? Helpful? Supportive? Patient? RJ had no idea where to start or how to compliment him for all the man had done for RJ. "Perfect," he finally admitted.

Stefan smirked. "Do you know how he feels for you?"

"He's told me."

Stefan lifted a leg and crossed it over a knee. Even for his age, he was still fit, tall like RJ with black hair that was gray at the temples, a silvery gray with slightly sharper features than RJ's, straight shoulders and a domineering presence, though he'd been nothing but gentle with RJ. Studying the older man, RJ could envision his future, and wasn't that put off by it.

"The question is, have you told him?"

"Me?" RJ cleared his throat when he choked.

"Well, I know Georgie's already half in love with him," Stefan teased. "Yes, you."

"There's a lot there." RJ flicked his gaze beyond Stefan, as uncomfortable again as he had been when they first arrived. He'd hoped the poke and prod of the visit wouldn't happen until later. Preferably not at all. "We have differences."

"And you're not willing to even try?"

"I didn't say that!" RJ straightened in his seat. "It's not like just agreeing on a living location. It's more than that."

"Okay, so what's stopping you?"

"The differences?" Eyebrows rose along with his voice.

Stefan nodded. "I heard you both. You're in stable situations, seem balanced enough to take it further. So what is stopping you?"

RJ leaned forward on his arms on the glass-topped table, picking at his fingernails. The umbrella over them fluttered lightly in the evening drafts. The silence stretched uncomfortably, mostly because he didn't know how to say it without sounding selfish.

"I'm not really in the place to offer advice, but I can listen," Stefan offered.

"He wants children," RJ whispered. "Adores them, and I'm not good parenting material. No offense, but you know my history, and while I didn't turn out to become a serial killer, I don't have a respectable background or childhood history. I was alone, my mother was an alcoholic and if it weren't for Grandma, I would have ended up in far worse shape than I am now, more jaded and likely in a less amenable situation across the board. You heard what he does. He gives everything for those kids. I can't take that away from him."

"And you feel admitting to how you feel will force him to abandon his wishes?"

"Or at the least, force him to choose, and I don't want that." RJ sighed, realizing the futility of it all. "So I haven't said anything, no."

"Don't you think he should be allowed to make that decision?" Stefan asked gently. "We all have choices in our lives. So many we regret, and so many that we wouldn't trade a moment for."

RJ knew that, but it didn't help him. "Honestly, if I could, I'd bring Tiffany home on a silver platter, give everything so he could see her just once."

"The girl he spoke of?" Stefan asked thoughtfully, his eyebrows knitting together as he listened.

"Yes. He loves her. Never said it openly, but I knew it and so did he. He was crushed when he came to me that Friday night after spending his last afternoon with her. Today, he finally smiled without that sadness. He's never down. It's not like him to be dark and brooding. That's my department." RJ grimaced. "So, I know I can't take away the option. Kids, or me? I'd give him the kids without a moment's hesitation, not because I don't love him, but because I do."

CHAPTER TWENTY

JULIAN STOOD frozen, the knife he held in his hand forgotten as he gaped, staring at the speaker on the wall.

"Oh, crap! I left that on again, didn't I?" David came over and tapped a button, silencing the soft-spoken words as they faded. David continued to scuttle around the kitchen, pulling things out of the pantry, ignorant of the private conversation Julian had accidentally overheard.

Julian didn't move an inch. His heart pounded like a jackhammer against his ribs. RJ loved him, and was holding himself back. Was willing to sacrifice himself for Julian's happiness. The knowledge made his throat dry. Absorbing it all, he set the knife on the cutting board to force his thoughts into line. He feared he was shaking too hard to dare to cut the peppers in front of him anyway. One slip and they'd be sautéing fingers instead.

He winced. *Bad image.* But it did the trick, bringing him mentally a few paces away from what he'd heard.

He loves me. Hearing RJ say it made his knees feel weak. Except... Julian frowned, realizing exactly what was going on. He gripped the counter edge with his palms, his mind whirling over the last bit he'd heard. Kids, or him? Not even a question. But from the sound of it, RJ didn't know that. He forced himself to focus. Cutting himself wasn't high on his list for the evening. Grasping the blade in firmer fingers, he attacked the peppers, cutting julienne strips for homemade stir-fry.

Yes, he'd do anything to see Tiffany, and the fact that RJ had read him so well... Seemed Ms. Johnston wasn't the only one to see right through him. He pinched his lips to hold in his sigh. Yes, he loved her, but she was gone. He had no idea which region of the adoption cycle she'd been shipped to, and that made his heart break all over again.

He couldn't even petition to adopt under his current circumstances. Single, in an apartment, and while it wasn't ideal and not what the adoption bureaucracy preferred, he *was* gay. He knew RJ's stance on kids, but even if Julian couldn't help change his mind, he would have RJ. At least, he hoped he would.

Obviously, they had a few things to discuss after this weekend. RJ may be willing to sacrifice himself for Julian's happiness, but he wasn't willing to accept it. Not by a long shot.

Thinking over the last few weeks, Julian had been spending more time at RJ's, staying over more nights, and even with Gregory, Charlie and Samson, it wasn't crowded. Most of the time, they were out and only home as a group in the late evenings. Julian actually liked the fullness of the house. He missed being around Toni, and his parents. The chaos felt normal, natural.

His brow twitched as he sliced, his thoughts picking up speed. No, he hadn't moved in fully. RJ was still nervous, and Julian was doing his best to coax him into the relationship.

But he just admitted he loved me. Though it wasn't to Julian, at least there wasn't a barren wasteland between them emotionally. Should he push a little harder? Was RJ ready if he did? If he brought his things over and said, I'm here? He scooped up the vegetables and dropped them into a waiting bowl.

Maybe he should bite the bullet and take the initiative, instead of treating RJ like he was wounded. This weekend was going a long way to help heal old hurts, whether he knew it or wanted it. Julian knew all about Toby, all about RJ's mother and now his father. Thankfully, Toby hadn't been back either. Julian had meant it when he'd said he'd deal with the other man. No one took swings at RJ.

"Julian." A tap on his shoulder broke into his thoughts. "You're going to overflow the bowl."

Julian blinked and realized David wasn't joking. "Sorry." He swept up the strips to add to the bowl, then turned to scrape the board over the sink. Standing at the counter, he quickly wrapped up the remaining veggies to put in the fridge. "What else do you need done?" He ran fingertips over the white granite tops, eyeing the chrome finish stove where the wok was already resting on a divot-cut grill plate made for the concave shape.

Someday, he'd love to have a kitchen like theirs. State-of-the-art appliances, brushed chrome and beautifully designed.

"Could you get the chicken out of the fridge? Other than that, it's just toss and stir."

Julian handed over the package.

"If you want, you can bring your things in. The room next to the den is yours for the weekend. Ours is upstairs."

"Okay. Thanks."

David nodded and Julian left for the car.

"THAT WENT very well," Julian remarked, lying beside RJ on their borrowed bed.

RJ snuggled against his shoulder. "For a first attempt, I'd have to agree. Maybe we can still be friends."

"Very generous of you," Julian stated drily.

RJ lifted over him to peer into his face. "What's that supposed to mean?"

"RJ, look at what he's done, what he's doing. He's offered his house, friendship, and has demanded nothing but given you both the chance to make amends on some level. Neither of you are guiltless in this situation."

RJ gaped with indignation. "But—"

"No, think about it. If it hadn't been for your mother, you never would have even tried to find him. You would have never known you were lied to. Knowing the truth for yourself was your responsibility."

Julian wasn't letting him claim even a little innocence in this matter.

He pushed up to create a small space over Julian. The sheet slid down his spine, creating shivers. "Picking sides?"

Julian shook his head. "Not about sides. You were both right, yet both wrong. Personally, I think you need each other."

RJ growled. "I don't need a father."

Julian inched fingers into his hair, caressing RJ's temple with languid circles of

184

his thumb. "Maybe, maybe not, but he's a person you could learn from, and that makes him invaluable as a friend."

RJ huffed, went to collapse, caught himself, then did it anyway. "I don't need you analyzing my every thought." He tugged the sheet back up, tucking it around them with jabs of stiff fingers.

"I'm not. Just thinking about tonight. And I've made some decisions."

RJ tensed. It was coming. The "It's not you, it's me" talk, or Julian saying he was bored and ready to move on. RJ was becoming a pro at these discussions.

"I haven't fully moved in, and I think that's been leaving you the wrong idea."

He wasn't unaware of that fact. RJ buckled down, preparing to hear the rest.

"When we get home, I'm going to take the next week to cancel my apartment and find storage for whatever I can't bring with me that I want to keep. It's time we made this real."

RJ jerked to brace himself over Julian. He was staring at the ceiling, but whipped to focus on RJ when he popped up.

"What?" he choked out.

Julian didn't blink. "I told you I was moving in, and tentatively you agreed, but I never followed through with it. Do you still want me there?"

RJ's mouth flopped open, then closed. "I thought you were the one taking your time."

"I was, but I think it was for the wrong reasons."

RJ shook his head and propped himself on an elbow. "Okay, back up and try this again.

What wrong reasons? And the halfway wasn't a problem."

"Babe, I love you. It's time you realized that. I was taking my time thinking after all you'd been through, you needed that, but I'm beginning to think I was wrong. I'm not saying I'm going to just steamroller my way into your life or into your home. I want us both to be ready, and I think you've been more ready than you've let me believe, or that I've wanted to see."

RJ studied him. "So you really want to shack up, as you put it?"

"Completely. Wanted it then, and even more now." Julian's fingers began caressing again.

RJ's heart skipped a beat. His throat tightened and he had to try twice to make his voice work. "But what about...things?"

"Like what? Spell it out, babe."

"Fine. The kids." RJ huffed. "I know what they mean to you."

Julian fell silent, examining RJ for several beats. Solemnly, he replied, "I won't lie to you, RJ. They do mean a lot, but babe, *you* mean everything. Being with you means we discuss and compromise. Being with me does not automatically mean I'm going to go out looking for a child to adopt, like a new set of sheets to buy. That's wrong in so many ways. We start with us first, or it doesn't matter what the intentions, there will never be a good foundation."

RJ couldn't fault that reasoning.

"I don't know where you got the idea that having children was more important than family—"

"Children *make* a family," RJ pointed out.

Julian's chuckle rocked them both. "No, babe. Us, you and I, we make a family. Children are added to family, even in a het relationship. Gregory and Charlie? I would consider them extended family, because they mean that much to you." Julian swept away a length of black hair that fell forward over RJ's face. "Even Stefan and David, they are part of the family that we make. Just you and me," he whispered. "And they surround us. That's family."

RJ swallowed. Instead of making him feel better, putting him at ease, this wasn't helping. He didn't understand the concept of *family*. He felt like he should. He knew his grandmother had loved him, and his mother had never resented him even though she'd all but drank herself to death, but the nonchalance behind Julian's explanation made his stomach twitch. RJ had no experience with what Julian was describing, which circled around once more to not being a good choice as a parent, as a father, to anyone. He didn't have the faintest clue how to do it.

"Babe?" Julian's fingertips were warm and tender as he passed through RJ's hair.

RJ sank to a bared shoulder, avoiding more. "I'm tired." Blatant evasion. He didn't care.

"Okay."

When he rolled over, Julian curled around him, holding him close, not pushing, not prying, and it made RJ feel worse. He knew he was hurting Julian and he couldn't stop it. Julian didn't deserve the silent treatment, not after that heartfelt attempt of an explanation, but he just didn't know how to deal with it.

How could he be good at something he'd never known?

CHAPTER TWENTY-ONE

JULIAN UNPACKED another load of clothes, separating them into the drawers RJ had emptied for him. All his hanging stuff was already in the closet. The apartment, as of thirty—he glanced at the alarm clock—thirty-eight minutes ago, was no longer his. It had taken closer to three weeks than one to get everything moved, packed and cancel the apartment, but it was done.

He wasn't regretting it, but he was worried RJ was. From living alone to suddenly having three more bodies and a dog in his house had to be unsettling. Watching him covertly as RJ hung his wash, Julian accepted it would take time for RJ to realize he meant this.

"Mom wants you to come to dinner," Julian mentioned.

"Did she say when?"

"Want to do the July Fourth barbeque?"

RJ flicked at a stubborn collar, then hung the shirt in the closet. "Sure."

"You won't be overwhelmed by all the strangers?"

"Probably, but I'll know you and Toni. I didn't spend a lot of time with your parents, but I'll remember them when I see them again." RJ repeated the shirt act three more times, ensuring collars were straight. Today was a lazy Saturday and they were both in shorts and T-shirts as they finished the last details of integrating their belongings. Julian loved RJ in shorts.

When Julian was done, he sat on the edge of the bed. "Babe?"

"Hm?" RJ had finished his shirts and was straightening the closet again.

"Is something wrong?"

RJ paused what he was doing, blinking owlishly at him. "No."

"You've been quiet since our weekend to Phoenix."

RJ sighed. "You can say Stefan's. I've had a lot to deal with, that's all."

Julian hated worrying, because he knew that. This had been a very rocky year for RJ.

"RJ, will you stop that for a minute and come here."

He shrugged. "Sure."

Julian captured a hand and brought him down to the bed with him. "Are you happy?"

"Yes, why?" Dark eyebrows crossed.

"With me being here?" Julian covered his hand on the bed. "If you're still uncomfortable..."

He left it hanging. Julian had thought they'd hammered this out, but as quiet as RJ had been over the last few days as they moved his stuff in and cleaned out the apartment, he just couldn't swear to it any longer.

"I'm not uncomfortable," RJ said quietly. "I like having you here, actually. It's nice having someone to come home to again. I adore Gregory and Charlie and honestly don't want them to leave unless they feel like they need to, but to have someone, you, here for now means the world to me."

"For now?" Julian couldn't believe he'd heard that right.

RJ's lips pinched, his gaze dropping like a stone.

"Shit," he hissed. "Now it makes sense." Julian slunk from the bed to kneel in front of RJ, his hand still clasped and not letting go. "Babe, RJ. I'm not leaving, not leaving you, not leaving here. I love you."

"So did Toby," he murmured tonelessly.

"Fuck. Him. Seriously. You do realize that we've already been together for most of six months, and I'm just now moving in to *your* place. I'm taking my time because I don't want to rush any part of this with you. I know he hurt you, and I know you've had shocks this year." He brought up RJ's chin, locking with his evasive gaze. "RJ, you better get used to the idea that I'm staying."

When a shaky shudder rocked RJ's body and he nodded, Julian's chest began to relax.

"Time, babe. I meant that." Ultimately, Julian wanted to make it permanent, but really didn't think RJ was ready for that large of a leap. Whether it was a ceremony like his friends had shared or something more low-key and private, he didn't care, but he had every intention of keeping the saucy man in front of him. Between his fear that Julian would leave and the certainty that he'd hate RJ for not being on the adoption train, Julian was at a loss.

The only way he could prove that RJ was wrong across the board was to stay, and he had no intention of doing anything else.

RJ'S CELL PHONE rang and when he spied the number he walked out to the patio and closed the door. His heart thudded when he silenced the ring and answered. It wasn't uncommon. He usually spoke in private when he was talking to his father, parts of him still raw but healing as the two men grew to know each other.

Stefan's strong voice filled the silence. "I found her."

RJ almost collapsed, but he sank into the patio chair instead, albeit shakily. "Where is she?"

"She's with a foster family in Pasadena. I've spoken with her placement agent, and I have permission to contact the family. Are you sure you want to do this, RJ? It will confuse her."

He rubbed stiff fingers over his forehead. "Honestly, Stefan, it just feels like something I need to do. I know he's been looking for her, though how you found her before he did, I don't understand."

"RJ," Stefan consoled kindly. "I have some powerful friends, and a few who owe me favors. You're positive he's been looking?"

RJ glanced over his shoulder, finding Julian in the kitchen working the magic that he was so good at. "He hasn't wanted me to know, but yes. He wants to find her to make sure she's safe and happy, or so that's what he's been telling himself. I know it's deeper than that. I miss her too," he finally admitted. "She's like sunshine. You'd understand if you met her."

"Okay. It will have to be a public meeting, and one of her foster guardians will need to be present."

"I understand." RJ hadn't expected anything less. "Just let me know when and where."

Once he was off the call, he sat with his elbows braced on his knees, his hands trembling midair as he tried to push away the misgivings that he was stepping in where Julian wouldn't want his help. Julian had been looking for Tiffany. Though he hadn't been vocal about it, RJ knew the underlying needs and worries. The hospital hadn't been forthcoming, not that it would even for a caregiver who'd been seeing to her recovery.

RJ knew Julian had been looking because he'd intercepted a phone message from an adoption center by mistake. It didn't take a genius to know what it was about or for whom.

An offhand comment to Stefan during one of their weekly phone calls had him offering to help as well. Doubting he'd be able to, RJ gave him the information. That had been four days ago.

RJ also knew this wasn't Julian going back on his word. But was it fair to Julian to let his fears continue to hold either of them back? RJ hadn't forgotten the young girl either, which had equally amazed and shocked him. Though Julian hadn't said more about children in the two months since he'd moved in with RJ, he had spoken about Tiffany. Reminisced about the time he'd spent with her at the hospital, and had mentioned his worries for her frequently. The inability to know for himself that his princess was safe, happy, and secure niggled at Julian's conscience. RJ was sure Julian hadn't brought up the fact that he was looking because he didn't want RJ to think he'd double-crossed his trust. RJ knew him well enough to see that. Even he was smart enough to recognize Tiffany wasn't just any child, but a child that had grown to mean the world to Julian. Whether he was a part of her life or not, Julian cared, and RJ loved that about him.

Since reconnecting with his father, RJ had had to face some very distasteful and rather unsavory truths about himself, his mother, and his grandmother's choices.

Julian had been right. He wasn't innocent to the life he led now. He'd had ample opportunity to find the man, but had let himself believe the stories they'd told him, that he'd had no way to know were lies. He should have done something when his grandmother had passed, tried to find him, tried to learn for himself just what had happened, but he hadn't. There was no one to blame but himself for that.

RJ really could have used the help rather than watching his mother lose job after job and having to work himself beyond school to make sure bills were paid. College had been hard enough. It was probably just as well that he wound up dropping out. He doubted he would have passed under the conditions he was in and financially, it was a nightmare. He was just grateful he had the chance, because he had found some of the strongest friends while there. He scrubbed over his face with a hand and slowly stopped trembling.

If he wanted his happiness, and he knew he wanted Julian happy, then it was time to do something about it, even if it meant tearing out his own heart to do it. He just prayed Julian would help patch him back together when he was done because he knew he didn't have the strength to do it alone. Steeling himself for the coming conversation, he rose from the chair and squared his shoulders.

Time to face some very dusty demons.

JULIAN WATCHED out of the corner of his eye as RJ talked out on the patio. He didn't intrude. He knew those calls were from Stefan. What bothered him was the stress RJ had been under the last few weeks. He didn't know what was causing it, and he refused to divulge. The man was like the Hoover Dam, only opening under great pressure, and even then it was in dribbles and leaks. The floodgate was locked tight. He just hoped when it finally gave that RJ lived through it.

He watched as RJ finished the call, and his heart went out to the other man. Something had been troubling him the last few days. Julian knew some of the stress was RJ becoming acclimated to having his father in his life again. The two men, though growing closer, were still finding their way.

RJ stood from the chair outside, his head hung like a heavy load was pulling at him, and Julian craved to hold him, to hear what was weighing him down so badly, or just to let him know he was there for him. But just as he began to reach for a towel to dry his hands from working over dinner on the stove to do just that, RJ twisted on a heel and came inside. He set his cell phone on the counter with a light, distracted motion.

"I have something I need to tell you."

Julian arched an eyebrow. "O-kay," he answered, hesitantly. Very rarely did anything good start out this way.

RJ steeled himself, then let it all out. "I'm not mad that you've been looking for Tiffany."

He held up a hand, halting Julian's immediate denial. *How did he find out?*

"I'm actually kind of glad that you were," RJ added softly.

"You are?" He did dry his hands on the towel then, tossing it on the counter. With an eye on the pans, he faced RJ.

"Since the barbeque at your parents', I've had a lot of thinking to do." RJ brushed the hair away from his face, slipping it behind an ear. A rued grimace twisted his lips. "It took some time to make heads or tails of what I felt, of how they treated me, made me feel. I've never met a boyfriend's family."

"Not even Toby's?"

RJ shook his head. "They don't live in California."

Julian remembered the day of the barbeque. His parents had greeted RJ like a family friend, and once they realized Julian had laid claim to the entrepreneur, they'd treated him like a son. It was a situation that had to be experienced rather than explained. It was what Julian had tried to create the image of that weekend in Phoenix, and RJ finally could see it in action. The fun, the support, the love, of family. The fact that Julian's parents had immediately included him without question didn't hit during that visit with so much going on that day, but was gradually wrapping around him and even though RJ may still not always understand, he was accepting, and that meant the world to Julian.

"Gregory's parents have always been friends because of Gregory. I adore his mother," RJ said. "But I don't know many parents like them."

"What does this have to do with Tiffany?" Julian was having a hard time following RJ's trail of zigzagging bread crumbs.

"I'm getting to that." RJ approached and laid a gentle hand on Julian's chest. He implored silently with his gray gaze, flitting from side to side, seeking, but for what Julian couldn't swear to. "Just hear me out and don't be upset."

"I doubt you'll upset me, babe," he replied, running tender fingers down his cheek.

"First, I've been foolish, on more than one count." When Julian's mouth popped open to argue, RJ touched his lips and shook his head. "Not yet," he entreated. Julian nodded, closing his mouth to listen.

"You've been the most patient man on the planet, not only for putting up with me, but for not demanding I get a grip and get over myself." He snickered crudely. "I would have, long before now. I don't even know any longer why I was so scared, to be honest." A gleaming warmth touched on his eyes. "I love you. I've known it and I've been an utter chicken shit to not tell you. And not fair to you either. I can't continue to ignore what I feel because I'm scared of what may come. I want now, and I want it with you. I love you."

"RJ, I knew you loved me," Julian soothed him gently, brushing fingertips over his jaw, maintaining a tingling contact that both craved. "I've seen it, and even if you haven't told me, I've known it." He wasn't about to admit to overhearing him those months ago. Not if he wanted to keep his nuts where they were. He'd held faith that RJ would realize what they both wanted could work, in its own way. It looked like he was going to be proven right after all.

Relief flickered, then swelled as tempting lips curled. The drawn look that had shadowed RJ's features since he'd walked into the kitchen evaporated. "I knew I was getting a smart man. I just hope the smart man can be forgiving."

He tilted to study RJ. "Why, babe?"

Licking his lips, he whispered, "Because I found her."

CHAPTER TWENTY-TWO

"PLEASE, DON'T be angry," RJ rushed when Julian gasped, literally staggering where he stood. "I heard a message on the voicemail and put it together."

Julian's lungs burned, and he realized he'd stopped breathing. Sucking in a jagged lungful, he asked, "You found Tiffany?"

"I didn't, no. Stefan did. I mentioned it and he asked if he could help. I didn't think he could and didn't see any harm in him trying. That's why he called. She's in Pasadena with a foster family."

Julian trembled. "Babe." RJ touched his face, freezing his mouth and his thoughts.

"I also know why you've been looking," he whispered.

His stomach turned into a collection of knots. "And that doesn't scare you?"

"Not like it did a few months ago. You were right. Having Stefan in my life has changed a few things for me. He's not trying to take over, or be something I don't need. He's being a friend, and he's a smart one, too," he mentioned with a light tone of self-aimed derision. RJ looped an arm around Julian's waist and he almost crumpled. "I know how you feel for her, and I don't blame you. I miss her, too."

"You do?" RJ nodded. "You understand?" He repeated his answer, black hair swaying like a swath of ink. Julian swept him up against his chest and made a half turn. "I can't believe it!" Setting RJ back on his feet, he studied his lover. "But...why the change of heart? You've been adamant and I was willing, so long as I had you."

RJ's eyes glistened. "Nothing is set in stone, least of all me. You've bent over backwards, putting up with me and I need to do my fair share to make this equal. Denying you this is something I can't do, and I never should have."

"RJ." Julian swallowed hard. "You know what I'm going to do next."

RJ blinked, apparently unprepared and taken off-guard by the seriousness of Julian's tone. "No."

Julian palmed his jaw and kissed him. A thorough, teasing temptation of tongue and lips. Showing the man how much he loved him with every touch, every caress.

The sizzle of a pan drew them apart and out of preservation of their dinner, Julian turned off the burners. RJ was panting when Julian released him. With both arms around Julian's middle, he held on and Julian relished the contact.

"I love you, and always will. I think there's more than enough love between us to share, if you're willing," Julian offered very gently, almost too scared to hope.

"I'm getting there." RJ lifted thick lashes to peer into his eyes. "I can't promise perfection, but I am willing to learn."

Julian smiled. "You know what this means?"

"Hm?"

"We'll have to make a commitment." Julian waited with a pounding heart, a tendril of fear sneaking into him. Neither had broached the subject, though Julian had always considered it a natural step of progression.

"Are you asking me to marry you?" RJ tipped his chin until he was staring eye to eye with Julian. He only wished he could read what the man was thinking in those gray pools.

"You're not against it, are you?" he asked.

"No."

"Then, yes, I'm asking."

"Asking what?"

RJ whirled out of his arms with a muted gasp. Julian raised his attention and discovered Charlie and Gregory standing a few feet away, watching on with curiosity.

"Didn't hear you come in," RJ mumbled.

"Not surprised." Charlie winked. "Smells good, Julian."

He cleared his throat. "Thanks." He tugged at RJ's waist, wanting an answer before any more distractions waltzed through the door.

"We can decide the logistics later, but would you—"

"Yes." Facing him again, RJ dug commanding hands into Julian's hair and brought them together, nose to nose and gaze to gaze. "Yes," he whispered against Julian's lips before kissing him senseless.

RJ STOOD WHEN a young woman entered the ice cream shop. He had an idea of what Tiffany's foster mother looked like, and he wasn't wrong when she zeroed in on him. A young brunette with medium brown hair in a ponytail, though it was the welcome in her eyes that gave her away.

"Karen?"

"Hi, RJ." She shook his hand. "Thanks for meeting me first like this."

"I understand. Believe me, if there's one thing I do understand, it's protocol."

Karen smirked. Playful blue eyes matched the humor in her voice. "Is Julian with you?" She glanced over his shoulder, following when he hitched a thumb toward the back of the shop where the restrooms were, a chuckle bubbling up. Poor Julian had been a wreck and had needed a few minutes by himself.

A moment later, Julian appeared and after introductions sat at the table with them. "I won't pull any punches. You'll both have to go through rigorous background checks and home inspections." She touched her hair, clearing her throat. "A gay couple has incredible scrutiny on them, but two in the same house, unrelated...it's not impossible, but she will have checks and interviews, and each in the house as well."

Both RJ and Julian nodded. "We are aware." Julian spoke clearly. "First, we both want to make sure she still wants to be with us. Her time at the hospital was stressful, and she may not feel the same. That's why we both wanted to visit first, though I will admit, just knowing she's in good hands makes a world of difference for me."

Karen patted Julian's hand. "She's happy, a little reclusive, shy, but that's to be expected under the circumstances. She's very brave, actually. Declined homeschooling."

Julian's beaming smile filled his face. "That's Tiffany," he stated with a smidgen of pride.

"She had good role models to help her through the worst of her recovery."

RJ covered Julian's hand when he blushed. His guy deserved every compliment for that.

"So, can we see her, to visit for today?" RJ was surprised that he was just as anxious, his chest tight and his skin clammy.

Karen nodded. She dug a phone out of her purse. "Bring her in, Doug."

Sitting so close to Julian, RJ felt his body vibrating with nervous energy. A moment later, the door's bell chimed and a man in his late twenties brought Tiffany in, holding her hand.

They both held their breaths. RJ knew because when she squealed and shot across the store straight for them, they both released with a whoosh.

"Julian! RJ!" She all but launched at them, each catching her with a stretched arm. Tables and chairs were no obstacle for a determined child.

"Hey, gorgeous." Julian gave her a squeeze.

RJ tapped her nose. "Hi, button." She snuggled in tighter.

It felt like forever before anyone wanted to let go.

JULIAN'S SMILE as they drove home warmed RJ in a way he'd never imagined.

"I can't say thank you enough, RJ."

There was a hoarse catch in his voice, giving away the deep emotion in those few, quiet words. RJ understood all too well. He had been a whirlwind of emotions since they'd arrived at the ice cream shop and during the hour after when they got to share ice cream cones with Tiffany and her foster parents. It was one of the best Saturdays he'd spent in a very long time.

Julian stared out the window, his chin pressed to a braced fist. He glanced across at RJ, who was driving. "Are you sure this is something you want to do? It's not something we can do halfway."

RJ twisted his hands on the steering wheel, selective vision keeping him from giving more than a passing glance to the other drivers on the road.

"Honestly, I'm scared shitless," he replied with a shaky laugh.

"That makes two of us," Julian offered quietly, though the happiness underneath it proved it was something he desperately wanted. A family of his own. With RJ.

"With you, I think I can do it. I know I want to," RJ whispered, his heart ricocheting into his chest as he made the final decision. After spending an hour with Tiffany—his sunshine— he could see why Julian wanted to take her under his wing. He remembered back to the afternoons he'd spent at the hospital with her, and could name what he'd been too scared, and even bullheaded, to examine.

The young angel had gotten under his skin. And the face she'd made him acknowledge, one of those dusty demons in his closet, hadn't been pretty, or easy to deal with and destroy. In many ways, finding Stefan had forced him to move forward. No one ever said doing it would be easy. But for Tiffany, he wanted to. *Amazing.*

"How do you think today went?"

Julian relaxed beside him. "Beautifully. Being the lone female in such a large group of uncles, she'll be spoiled rotten."

"There will be your mother, and I'm sure Gregory's. And Pamela."

Julian's eyes closed as he rested his head on the seat. He reached a hand across the console and laid a flat palm to RJ's thigh. "Love you," he said in utter contentment.

"Love you too," RJ replied, making plans and not worrying about the coming upheavals and challenges. They would come no matter how much he didn't want them. They'd face them and move on. He loved the man at his side too much to hold either of them back another minute.

His lips twitched. *I'm going to have a daughter.* The thought didn't fill him with terror or dread the way it had that very first time Julian had admitted to his love of children. Seeing Tiffany's smiles, hearing her laughter, meant more to him than he'd ever dreamed. It may not be every child; she definitely had reached him and from what others had said, he'd done the same for her. In many ways, he needed her as much as she needed a loving family to call home. Through Julian, with Stefan's help, he could see it, could *see* that part of himself and embrace it, rather than running scared or denying the need.

I know I wasn't the best son, Mom, but I will be the best dad I can.

He rested a hand over Julian's, giving him a light squeeze, holding him until they were home.

EPILOGUE

One year later

"HAPPY BIRTHDAY, dear Tiffany, happy birthday to you!" The backyard chorus was loud and boisterous with the menagerie of vocal battles, female, male, and canine added to the mix.

Julian centered the large white iced cake on the covered picnic table, nine candles lit for the princess of the hour.

"Happy birthday, princess." He pressed a kiss to her temple. "Make your wish and blow them out."

Her cute face went solemn as she whispered her wish, then hauling in a lungful of air, blew for all she was worth. The candles didn't stand a prayer.

Cheers and applause broke the silence, starting the lab and two greyhounds into another raucous rendition of accolades again.

With the backyard filled with streamers, balloons, people, dogs, tables and food, there was barely a foot to move, but RJ didn't mind. It had been a rocky year and then some since that visit at the ice cream shop. Court visits, Child Services, and enough red tape to line the California coast. Though he didn't mind at all seeing Karen and Doug when they came by.

Those were good visits because sometimes they had Tiffany with them.

He let out a contented sigh, feeling fulfilled in a way he'd never dreamed. A wandering stare snagged with his dad's, and he smiled. Stefan toasted him in return with a raised glass of punch, David at his side. The two grandpas had come for the weekend, decreeing there was no way they would miss their only granddaughter's birthday.

RJ shifted when a body sidled up to him. "So, how's fatherhood?" Charlie gave him a cheeky grin.

He chuckled with amusement. "Not all that bad."

"Three months Monday, right?"

RJ nodded. "Yeah." He couldn't believe it himself. "How are you two doing? We miss you not being here."

"Miss you guys too." Charlie gave RJ a light shoulder bump.

Gregory had landed a sweet university community rental property with a pool less than a mile from the beach. It took him longer to get to work and for Charlie to get to class, but neither man seemed to mind. As much as RJ hated to see them go, they all knew it was needed to bring Tiffany home, and though it was never said, RJ thought Gregory was ready to make things a little more permanent between himself and Charlie. RJ was just waiting for the announcement from Gregory.

"I'm surprised Greg's mom didn't just bring her a pony. She brought her everything else." Charlie nodded toward the stack of wrapped presents that Tiffany was just beginning to make a dent in.

"Well, grandmas have that right," RJ teased in return, well aware that they all had a hand in that colorful mess beside Tiffany. They watched as another gift was plunked down on her lap, both shaking their heads ruefully as the pile of loot stacked up. "She's going to need another shelf, at least." Her squeals of delight and laughter filled the backyard.

He was ecstatic to see her open and not at all shy with any of her new "extended family" as they all shared in her birthday. The fact that RJ's circle of friends had more uncles than aunts didn't bother her either. She'd accepted their relationship with a stoic calmness, and she'd transferred that same acceptance to each and every one of her "uncles". Tiffany had even surprised them during one of their early neutral visits that she knew what it meant to be gay, and that it didn't bother her. Two dads were just as good for her, especially if they were Julian and RJ. She would also be starting at a new school in the fall, but she said she was ready. There was a lot of strength and courage in that pint-sized bundle of energy.

When warm arms circled his waist from behind, RJ felt his knees go weak.

"Hi, sexy." The words rumbled into his ear with a private caress.

RJ cupped Julian's left hand, the thin gold bands catching when he did. The two men hadn't gone as lavish as Josh and Laurence's wedding, the very night RJ and Julian were first tossed together, but instead had held a solemn commitment ceremony over the holidays. Everyone had been invited. They'd even asked Karen and Doug if they would like to come. When they agreed, RJ and Julian had asked if Tiffany could be a part of the ceremony. Their princess had been so excited, she'd danced on her toes the entire day of the event. They did everything they could to start including her in their lives, and in the end it had helped her transition go a lot smoother.

When Karen busted him gazing softly at his daughter as she tore into another gift with abandon at the other end of the table, Karen winked with a broad smile of approval. He chuckled, knowing he was grinning like a proud papa. How could he not?

RJ cleared his throat. "What did she wish for?"

"Are you ready for this?"

"Depends. Is it going to break the bank?" Though neither man was against spoiling her, they were against frivolous money spending and knew teaching her the difference would pay off in about seven years. Or so they hoped.

"Nope. She wished for us to stay together, to be her family. I don't think it's sunk in that she's staying."

"That is sweet," Charlie warmly stated.

"Just think, next year, the adults will probably be outnumbered by kids because she'll have friends to invite."

"I don't know, RJ," Charlie said. "There's a lot of people here who aren't going to miss a day if they can help it. Greg's mom was as excited as Tiffany, I think. She only had Jay and Greg, and Jay and Libby haven't given her any grandkids yet."

"I hear my name."

RJ smiled at one of his closest friends as Gregory came to stand beside Charlie.

"Can't believe you're the doting father," Gregory teased RJ.

RJ tossed his head. "Yeah, well, couldn't believe you were gay."

"Oh, ouch," Julian joked, wincing at the playful jabs.

"Good point." Gregory looked toward Tiffany with genuine admiration. "She's awesome. I wish you both the best of luck, and if you ever need it, I'm very scary for possible boyfriends. She's going to have them by the busload." A turquoise headband kept her blonde hair away from her face, doubling the sparkle in her eyes whenever she looked up at RJ and Julian.

"I know," Julian groaned, still holding on to RJ. He heard the happiness and a total lack of worry in Julian's answer. "She's already talking cheerleading and who knows what it'll be by school. She's only going into the fourth grade. Can you imagine high school?" Julian shuddered in playful horror.

"She's a survivor, our girl," RJ whispered.

"Her dads aren't half bad either," Julian said into his ear for RJ alone. "We've come a long way." He dropped a kiss behind Julian's ear, then let him go. "So glad I got you."

"Me too, babe." RJ sighed.

"Daddy RJ! *Daaaad!*" Tiffany's squeal carried easily.

Both men took the moment in stride. "What, button?"

"Look what I got!"

"I think that's her way of saying she's been ignored for our cuddles long enough," Julian whispered.

RJ chuckled. He wasn't alone in his laughter as they approached their daughter to enjoy in her exuberance. Sitting on either side of her, they shared in her laughter and that of their family and friends until the cake was nearly gone, the ice cream was more melted than not and even the dogs were burgered out.

It was a day of wonderful memories for RJ, and they were just beginning for him and his family.

ABOUT THE AUTHOR

Diana DeRicci is the sexy, flirty pen name of Diana Castilleja. A romance author at heart, DeRicci's writing takes you into a saucier spectrum of sensuality and sexual adventure, where a happily-ever-after is still the key to any story. Diana lives in Central Texas with her husband, one son, and a feisty little Chihuahua named Rascal. You can catch the latest news on all of Diana DeRicci's writing and books on her website. Feel free to drop Diana an email. She'd love to hear from you.

Visit her on the web at:
www.DianaDeRicci.com

PURPLE SWORD PUBLICATIONS, LLC
www.purplesword.com